Penguin Books

an open swimmer

Tim Winton has published twenty books for adults and children, and his work has been translated into twenty-five languages. Since his first novel *An Open Swimmer*, won the *Australian/*Vogel Award in 1981, he has won the Miles Franklin Award four times (for *Shallows*, *Cloudstreet*, *Dirt Music* and *Breath*) and twice been shortlisted for the Booker Prize (for *The Riders* and *Dirt Music*). He lives in Western Australia.

CANCELLED

TIM WINTON

an open
swimmer

PENGUIN BOOKS

PENGUIN BOOKS

Published by the Penguin Group
Penguin Group (Australia)
250 Camberwell Road
Camberwell, Victoria 3124, Australia
(a division of Pearson Australia Group Pty Ltd)
Penguin Group (USA) Inc.
375 Hudson Street, New York, New York 10014, USA
Penguin Group (Canada)
90 Eglinton Ave East, Suite 700, Toronto, ON M4P 2Y3, Canada
(a division of Pearson Penguin Canada Inc.)
Penguin Books Ltd
80 Strand, London WC2R 0RL, England
Penguin Ireland
25 St Stephen's Green, Dublin 2, Ireland
(a division of Penguin Books Ltd)
Penguin Books India Pvt Ltd
11, Community Centre, Panchsheel Park, New Delhi-110 017, India
Penguin Group (NZ)
67 Apollo Drive, Rosedale, North Shore 0632, New Zealand
(a division of Pearson New Zealand Ltd)
Penguin Books (South Africa) (Pty) Ltd
24 Sturdee Avenue, Rosebank, Johannesburg 2196, South Africa

Penguin Books Ltd, Registered Offices: 80 Strand, London WC2R 0RL, England

First published by Allen & Unwin 1982
First published in paperback by Picador 1983
Published by McPhee Gribble/Penguin 1991
This edition published by Penguin Books Australia Ltd 1998

13 15 14

Cover design by Ellie Exarchos © Penguin Group (Australia)
Typeset in 10/12 pt Bembo by Midland Typesetters, Maryborough, Victoria
Printed and bound in Australia by McPherson's Printing Group, Marborough, Victoria

National Library of Australia
Cataloguing-in-Publication data:

Winton, Tim, 1960– .
An open swimmer.

ISBN 978 0 14 027402 8.

I. Title.

A823.3

penguin.com.au

FSC
www.fsc.org
MIX
Paper from
responsible sources
FSC® C001695

This book is for John and Beverley Winton,
two of my best friends.

ACKNOWLEDGEMENTS

I would like to offer my thanks and respect to Michael Henderson and Denise Fitch for their patience and assistance in the writing of this book.

The lines from 'Diving into the Wreck', from *Diving into the Wreck: Poems 1971–1972*, by Adrienne Rich, copyright © 1973 by W.W. Norton & Company, Inc., are reprinted by permission of the author and W.W. Norton & Company, Inc.

I am she: I am he

whose drowned face sleeps with open eyes
whose breasts still bear the stress
whose silver, copper, vermeil cargo lies
obscurely inside barrels
half-wedged and left to rot
we are the half-destroyed instruments
that once held to a course
the water-eaten log
the fouled compass

We are, I am, you are
by cowardice or courage
the one who find our way
back to this scene
carrying a knife, a camera
a book of myths
in which
our names do not appear.

'Diving into the Wreck', Adrienne Rich

prologue

It had been a long fight between Jerra Nilsam and the fish. He pressed the flat end of the oar against its brow. Globes of moisture clustered on its flanks. His father grinned in the stern. The engine was chuckling. Water parted like an incision behind. The fish grunted. His father said it was a turrum. The long fan of tail slapped the gunwhale, the gills were pumping, and blood globbed the bottom of the boat.

In the water, the black diamond, the mate, cruised. When he had gaffed the turrum over the side, cuffed on the chin by the tail, the diamond had been there, silver when the sun caught its flanks.

Chuff-chuff, the turrum was grunting. Looking up at him, the eye never blinked. The fish began to thresh, clenching and unclenching. Jerra kept the oar hard over its brow, near the gaff-hole. His palms were bleeding and he wanted to cry. He grinned back at his father.

The diamond curved and straightened, blemishing the surface with its scalpel of a dorsal fin. He wished they had a bigger engine.

Bashing. It was bashing the gunwhale. The fish buckled up, almost out of the boat. He fell on it, hugging, feeling the fin spikes in his chest. With a spastic twitch it deflated, mumbling.

'It's dead,' his father said.

He let go and sat up with glistening scales on his chest and glistenings on his cheeks.

He looked over the side. The diamond had gone.

'Want to open it for the pearl?'

'No.'

'It might have one.'

'I don't want to cut him up, Dad.'

He wished they had a bigger engine and that the fish would be alive again.

PART ONE

the bush

Away to their left, a flight of cockatoos lifted from the gums and swung in a pink cloud over the road and into the bush.

'Petrol?' Sean asked.

'Enough if we find something soon.'

'Bloody tourist maps.'

'Not far. Road's headin' for the coast.' Jerra glanced at Sean, whose pale curls bobbed in the breeze from the open window. He flicked on the beams, lighting up the loose surface ahead.

The road was sloping away, curving, unknotting itself. He saw the thick red tail of gravel dust lifting in the mirror.

'Shaking hell out of the ol' bus,' he said.

'Wonder it's stayed together this long.'

'Be still going long after we're skinned and dried.'

The headlights caught the eyes of animals and held them by the throat, rigid, until they passed in a clattering rush of stones and dust.

A roo floated across, bashing off into the undergrowth.

'Shit, Jerra!' Sean slid back, clutching at his seat belt.

'Had plenty o' room.'

'Should have a roo-bar on this thing. That would've put us in the heap for good.'

'Okay if you can afford it.'

Sean shrugged. Jerra hit the horn.

'The roos'll know we're coming now.'

'Great.'

'Be setting up in the dark.'

'Don't talk about it.'

'Remember that time out past Eucla?'

Sean reached over and smacked the horn. Jerra laughed.

'That's for bloody Eucla and the torch batteries.'

Jerra bashed the horn with his elbow.

'That's for the look on your face in the morning.' Already, he smelt crushed insects and the flaky wood under ghost gums. 'The great outdoorsmen!'

Eventually, gravel gave way to sand and banksias and black, fallen marri trunks. The track wound down the rutty slope. The springs groaned as they dropped a wheel into a washout.

'Good for the diff,' said Jerra.

Grass swished along the chassis as Jerra pulled out of the rut. The track cleaned up for a bit, doodling off from side to side, further, deeper. At a flat, clear spot, they came upon an old corrugated shack.

'Ex-residence,' said Sean, noting it. Needlessly, Jerra thought.

Further down, swelling out of the carved-off bank of the track, was a grizzled she-oak with the letters NO pared neatly out of the bark, the O bleeding viscous sap from the white flesh.

The sand was getting whiter and softer, and Jerra pushed through a few soft sections, feeling the VW glide and whip; he flicked the wheel a bit harder than was needed, but it was soft and he didn't know when he might be caught without enough speed.

A clearing. They rattled into the grove, scattering a few rabbits caught in the light. Jerra switched off. There was only the gums and the sea.

Sean dropped a mallee root onto the fire. Jerra rolled the pan. He flipped the stuff onto the plate.

'Here.'

They ate the buttery fried eggs breathing and talking around the food in their mouths.

'Bit of a turn-up. First time we've ever struck camp without pitchin' on a nest of ants – '

'Or a cocky's driveway – '

'Rifle range – '

'Creekbed – '

'All we need now is to make friends with a possum with the clap – '

'Oh, geez, 'ere he goes!'

They pissed and went to bed. The smell of smoke in his clothes made Jerra feel he had been there for ever.

the distant
mutterings of gums

In the daylight, the clearing was another place. Last night it had been as big as a paddock, now there was just enough room to turn the VW.

Poking the ground with their spears, they turned over the leafy crust, revealing a moisture which could survive the heat. The musty damp clung to the soles of their feet.

'Fire's nearly out,' Jerra said, dropping the gear in the shade.

Sean scuffed his feet into the leaves. Jerra went for some wood.

The fire nipped at their knees, spitting. Jerra sat feeling the roughened edges of his hands.

'Sore?'

'Just not used to it. Haven't used 'em for ages. Never liked peelin' leatheries, anyway. Dad always used to do it.'

'Yeah, your Dad.'

'S'pose he did most things for me, eh?'

'Yeah.'

'How's your ol' man?' Jerra asked as if he was interested. Probing.

'Into Westam at the moment.'

Catching red emperors, thought Jerra. From the boardroom table.

'Westam?'

'Yeah,' said Sean.

Fat congealed, the fire subsided. The late breeze was in when they awoke, sprawling on the thick foam mattress, sucking teeth, farting, hearing the gums bend and unbend.

'Slept in this ol' bus a few times,' said Sean, peering through the sparse hairs on his chest, letting out a long bark.

Jerra gazed at the insect squash-marks on the ceiling, ran his finger through the patina of gravel dust.

'Lots.'

'How many trips?'

'Lost count.'

'Wish you'd stop farting.'

Jerra grinned. It was like lying in the park after school. He could feel the flat leaves of clover under him, see the scabby trunk above bearing all the open-mouthed maggies that chased them to and from school, and he rubbed the little scar on his thumb.

Shadows appeared on the granite spill. Black holes and shafts opened and wavered. Jerra and Sean hopped and stumbled out to the headland. Within an hour there would be no daylight. A breeze tumbled in cool ripples from the sea, and gulls bumped in the currents, up, around behind them as they stepped out to a smooth ledge and began at the tangles:

> *loop*
> *under,*
> *side,*
> *pull through,*
> *BUGGER!*

. . . bite it off half-way.

'Should've put this bait in water,' Sean said.

'Ooh, ripe.' Jerra flicked his baited hook out. 'A cast at last.'

'Rhymes.'

'Eh?'

Squatting on the warm, grey rock, they felt the air cooling towards twilight. You could feel it, next to the water. A peculiar smell, wet granite. Dark as the distant mutterings of the gums.

Against the small flanks of stone came the glugs and laps of the dark water.

The nylon was light on their fingers, rising and falling in the drowsing swell.

'Fish,' murmured Jerra.

'Hmm?'

'Catching an' eating the buggers.'

'Why else would you sit on a rock getting a sore bum?'

Jerra looked into the greenish-black.

'Dunno.'

'Only good when there's something down there interested in getting hooked.'

'Arr.'

'Easier at a fishmarket.'

'Eating's only half of it. Less.'

'It's something.'

'The waiting. Like this.'

'Bloody frustrating.'

'Like when we were younger and Dad took us. His fault when I didn't get anything.' Jerra remembered the endless mornings anchored on a mirror-calm stretch of water, when Sean was like a real blood-brother to him, when there was nothing but herring on his mind.

'He never missed a bite.'

'Hated him for it. Wish you could fix up the dumb things you do when you're young.' He was unsure what he was really saying. He wondered what Sean was thinking.

'Getting dark.' Sean had packed his gear. 'Let's go.'

'What's that?'

'What?' said Jerra.

'On the beach.'

Jerra stopped walking and peered in the bad light.

'Looks like a dog or something with four legs.'

'Probably a wild one from up the bush.'

It was gone and so was the light.

Dark. They lit the fire. Something mushy was fired in a can, and they sucked tea from tin mugs, spitting tea-leaves into the fire. Bloody tea-bags; Jerra knew they were around somewhere, but he gave up and they brewed it in the billy. They went to bed as the dew came settling on their backs.

In the night, Jerra woke to the sounds of movement outside. The food was safe. It was probably the dog they had seen. He slept.

Before dawn, Jerra climbed over Sean and went stiffly out into the half-light and the long, crackling wild oats. Dew was ice between his toes, the breeze roughened the skin of his shoulders. He tossed a few sticks on the warm ash, pulled on a shirt, and went down to the beach.

He scuffed along the sheltered meniscus of the shore. In the middle of the bay, waves peeled off in long, smooth folds, crumpling onto the banks, spray wafting from the crests as the swells flexed and collapsed on themselves, rumbling.

There were footprints and scuff-marks in the sand, he noticed. Handprints not footprints. Something had been carved into the sand, but the tide had softened it to a few grooves and channels in the mushy shore.

After breakfast they argued over the swell, avoiding each other's face.

'Come *on*! This is the first surf we've had for ages.'

'Thought you wanted some fish,' said Jerra, dropping the hessian bag.

'Fish are always there,' said Sean. 'The swell might be gone tomorrow.'

They stood kicking the dirt with the balls of their feet until Jerra shoved the diving bag under the car in surrender.

'You can go diving if you like.'

'Better stay together.'

Brilliance held the lids against their eyes. Sun beat them into the sand. Gulls slid about as they paddled out and sat in the rolling shimmer, straining their necks, watching for the sets that bumped up on the horizon, the biggest feathering early and a long way outside. That sink and pull in the guts. They fidgeted in that time between seeing the horrie begin to break and deciding where to wait. In the midst of the set, swells back and ahead, there was no horizon, no beach, only the shush of water falling from the crests and the aqua fluting of the hollow troughs.

They felt the breeze and the bite of spray. It seemed a long way to walk back when they could paddle and take off no more.

Half-way back along the beach, a beam protruded from amongst the crackling weed and sand.

'This'd be good on the fire,' said Sean.

'Jarrah, too. Burn like hell.'

'Here,' said Sean, kneeling on the hot sand.

They pulled at the exposed end. Nothing would move it.

'A hell of a long way up the beach to be buried that deep.'

'You know the weather in July this far south.'

'Plenty of wood near camp.'

'Yeah,' said Jerra. 'Not as if we have to excavate fossil fuel.'

Flinging their boards to the ground in the shade of the Veedub, they might never have been wet.

For tea that night, they ate long slabs of sweep and thick abalone steaks prised from the reef, the fire throwing a pale, flesh-coloured circle, a wavering ripple in the black bush.

'Thought what you're going to do?' Sean blinked, his eyes lit red. To Jerra, sometimes, they were like the eyes of a fox drilled in a spotlight.

'Ah, who knows?'

'Have to decide, eventually.'

'How does a bloke decide, these days?'

'I never had much trouble.'

'You were set. All you had to do was get old enough. Yer biggest hassle was buying the blue tie.'

'Hardly.'

Jerra smelt the singed hairs on the back of his hand. He felt that deadness in him when he felt like picking up something heavy, an axe or something, and heaving it into the ocean, just to hear the splash.

'That job with your old man was waiting for you.'

'So is yours.'

'Ah, bullshit.' It really was, he thought. They all feed you bullshit.

'Just a matter of growing up. They were all expecting you to finish at Uni.'

'Who?'

'Your oldies and your grandfather. He put a lot of time into you, you know.'

'Hey, how come you're so respectable all of a sudden?'

'You grow up.'

'When you get a job.'

'Yes.'

'Yes.' When you get a job. Jerra remembered the first day Sean went to work, crisp and aloof. It wasn't long afterwards that he left to live in a townhouse in South Perth subsidised by the corporation.

Jerra let the feeling of it pass over him as all those things did now.

'Ah, come on.'

'You'll see.'

'I do now.'

'Everyone goes through it.'

'Through what?'

'You know what I mean.'

'Like getting pubes on yer dick.'

Sean smiled, shaking his head.

'Mine are still there,' said Jerra. 'How's yours?'

'That's piss-weak.'

'Talk about something else then.'

'Given in to corruption, have I?'

'Ah, I dunno, Sean.'

'You gotta live,' said Sean, tossing a sappy log into the flames.

Jerra turned from the smoke.

Sean slung the tepid tea into the bush. The moon was a pale splash on the bay.

He lay still. Sean breathed steadily. Outside, sap hissed in the veins of the green log. Bitter smoke seeped into the van, clouding the windows. The breeze strengthened. Only vaguely could he see the shadows of the bitching trees, contorted in the moonlight.

Just as Jerra was about to sleep, Sean rolled onto his side and said, 'Mum.' He would never have said it, awake.

Jerra could have hit him. He was awake for quite a while after that. It scared the hell out of him, and he couldn't help but wonder how much Sean knew.

An animal coughed in the night, hacking indifferently.

a skeleton with
the eyes still in it

There were clouds, and a chill that hung at the base of the trees. Jerra rekindled the fire. Sour ash had sunk into the earth under the dew; sun appeared briefly in a gap in the grey above the hills. A stunted swell struggled through the flecked and flattened surface of the ocean, onto the sandbar, silent, feeble.

'Wonder if there's a spring around here,' Sean asked idly, later in the morning. 'Water's getting low.'

'Nothing on the map,' said Jerra, feeling the ribbed contours on the inside of a shell.

'That means stuff-all, doesn't it? This place isn't even on the map. Only things that are are Perth and Kalgoorlie.'

'Well, there's odds to say we're not at either of those.'

A squabbling flight of gulls blew overhead.

'Bloody seagulls,' said Jerra. 'Just follow you round, waiting for you to drop something.'

'They gotta survive.'

'Bloody scabs.'

Out of the corner of his eye, Jerra saw Sean watching him.

The track was flanked by high, rubbery dune scrub. Further into the hills, the trees reduced the wind to a rumour in the treetops. Tracks of small animals showed riddles in the sand. Birds, tiny blurs, flitted across the track.

'Further than I thought,' said Jerra, oozing sweat.

'We'll end up at one of those two dots on the map.' Sean

dragged the jerrycan through the sand. 'Gawd knows what the bloody hell we're doin' this for.'

Up ahead, a log in the shade of a rattling wattle.

The log was rough and wobbly. Through the jagged leaves, sunlight mottled their skin. The bay stretched away, a hook, brilliant in the intermittent sun. Inlets and coves melted into the haze. The sea boiled on the cliffs. The Cape loomed like another continent.

They didn't say anything. The sweat and the view let Jerra relax for a moment, and for that moment, it was like it had always been before, with nothing in his head that wouldn't fit.

Jerra thumped his mate. He *was* his mate. The log wobbled. The dry leaves of the wattle shook.

NO, said the tree as they passed. Jerra ignored it cheerily.

Tough grass grew through the fissures in tin and timber, worming up under the boarded windows, and trees had elbowed their way in through the roof, flexing, bending upwards and out, growing inside and almost ready to lift the roof off. Grass penetrated the crust of the truck. Holes in the roof left warm pools on the fermenting upholstery. Jerra saw. It was like the hulks he had seen gaping in the bush where he had wandered after school, watching carefully for snakes and spiders and dirty things. It would have made a good hideout, with holes to shoot through and bayonet the Japs. A good hideout, he thought, guiltily. He still looked for hideouts, despite his age.

'God,' he whispered. 'It looks like a skeleton with eyes still in it.'

'You can hear it rusting.'

All was intact, but disintegrating.

Behind the shed, the water-tank was rusted through at the rim. Jerra thumped it. Little freckles flaked off. Gutters fallen into the undergrowth, the rain had continued to fill, falling through the rusted cover.

Jerra felt the cold greenish tap. A stack of bottles winked green and brown.

'Hey, you reckon we should be knocking it off like this?'

'No one's been here for ages. Who's gonna mind?'

'You mean who's gonna know.'

'Ah, come on, hold the can.'

It filled with a cold, loud rush. Jerra tightened the spout.

'Here, grab an end.'

'Nuh-uh. Not in the contract. I carried it up.'

'Rotten bugger.'

'It's downhill.'

NO the she-oak was congealing.

'Shall we add an S and a T?'

'Waffor?' asked Jerra, pulling the jerrycan, trying not to notice it.

'SNOT.'

Jerra looked at him and gave him a kick. 'Don't let the employees hear you saying things like that. Give 'em the impression you're the wrong kind of material.'

During lulls in the flames, shadows creased their lips, holes opened where eyes had been. Sean farted and stretched.

'Really quite full.'

'Shows how hungry a bastard can be, when he can eat baked beans and nearly admit to enjoying it.'

'Don't get any better, do they?'

Sean burped a long bark, 'Rrruth.'

'Definitely.'

'My bladder creaketh.'

'Piss.'

'If I must.'

'Must or bust.'

'Back in a sec.'

'Watch the possums. Never know what you might catch.'

'They should be worryin'.'

Things breathed in the fire. Carefully, Jerra watched the dew appearing. It came silent on the rocks, on the softness of grass, on sticks, ropes, beading brown on the blade of the axe and, unless you watched for it, it came without your knowing. Until you moved. Or ran a hand over something. He chafed his hands together over the fire.

Twigs and leaves moved.

'That was quick.' He turned.

It wasn't Sean.

'Shit!' he cried, almost going into the flames. 'Who the hell – '
He saw fire in the beard and eyes.

'Where you from?' the old man asked.

'The city,' Jerra admitted.

'Campin', eh?'

'Where you from?' Jerra asked, tremulously.

'Around.' A vague wave.

'A shack?' He was choking.

'And tank.'

'Oh, Gawd, we ah – '

'Nobody got claim on the clouds. Least not me.'

'Just thought – '

'It's orright.'

Fire twisted. The blood cracked in his ears.

'Well – '

'Would've scared youse off.'

Undergrowth parted.

'Ah, thought I took a wrong – '

'Sean, this is someone from up the hill.'

Sean was stiff.

'Hey look, we didn't take anything. The old joint looked – '
Jerra sat over the fire. It burnt his cheeks.

'Doesn't matter,' said the old man, squatting in the warm. Sean began to say something, but Jerra silenced him with a showing of teeth.

Rims of water glistened in the old man's eyes. His cheeks were red in the firelight.

'Smoke?'

Sean shook his head ungraciously.

'Sorry,' said Jerra. 'Don't smoke.'

'Gawd. Nothin' to be sorry about, son. Bastards 'ave never done me any good. Jus' more pins in the b'loon. Still, they're somethink.'

A doughy wad was rolled across the palms, fingers the colour of scorched twigs. A rolling tongue followed the movement.

'Put the billy on, Sean. We'll have a brew.'

Jerra watched the tobacco rolled into a brittle sliver of paper. There was print on both sides.

'How do you like your tea?' asked Jerra.

'To chew, like real baccy. But as a bev'ridge – dark an' black.'

'Sugar?'

'Nah. Rots yer guts.'

Jerra smiled faintly, picking the black bits out of the powdered milk.

'Thought it was teeth.'

'No problem there.'

Sean lowered the billy into the flames. Drops on the outside turned to steam.

'How long you been here?'

'Maybe twenty years, give or take a war.'

'In the shack all that time?'

'That an' the shed on the beach.'

'On the beach?' said Sean. 'There isn't one on the beach.'

'Gone.'

'Where?' asked Sean.

'Burnt down. A long while back.'

The old man was looking right into the orange twists. He drew out a stick, lit it, watching the flame all the way up to his face and back.

'What sort of paper is that?' asked Jerra.

'Bible.'

'Eh?'

'Ran out of papers. Years ago. Still 'ad a couple of old Gideons we knocked off from a fancy motel. Last one, this. Only just warmin' up on it. You cut 'em up the columns and whack off a few verses.'

It stank. Jerra tried not to grimace.

'Where you up to?' grinned Sean.

The old man chuffed smoke. You could hear him suck on the paper.

'Deuteronomy. Eighteen? Nineteen. Tough goin'. Cities 'n rules. Verse thirteen: *You shall be blameless before your God*. Fourteen: *For these nations . . .* er . . . bugger, I can't remember.' He kneaded the hard of his crusty hands. 'What do you do for a livin', son?'

'I'm a clerk,' said Sean. 'Of sorts.'

'For a company, eh?'

'Yeah, sort of.'

Jerra made a face.

'School before that?'

'Uni, actually.'

'The Uni, eh?' The old man grinned. 'They tell yer anything at the Uni?'

'I majored in history.'

'History. Learn a pack from the past. Yer can too. Ever learn you anythink?'

Sean looked into the fire, lips compressed. Heat ticked in the billy. Wisps weaved through holes in the lid. The old man looked at Jerra.

'I'm out of work.'

'Got a trade?'

'No. But I've worked on the fishing boats back along the coast, last year. Things got a bit rough. A tough season. I got laid off.'

'Yeah,' sighed the old man. 'Things'd be rough. Like the boats?'

'It was rough. But okay. I liked the fish.'

Sean, perched on his log, rolled his eyes, scalloping a hole in the dirt with his heel.

'Ah, yeah,' said the old man scuffing his hands together, little greenish flecks of tobacco catching in the hard cracks. He expanded a little. 'Fish. The things a fish'd know, eh?'

'Yep.'

'Know anythink about fish?'

''Bout all he does know,' said Sean.

'Yeah,' said Jerra, ignoring the sarcasm. After all, it was true enough.

'What about one f'every letter of the alphabet?'

'He can do two at least.'

The old man looked at Sean.

'Can he now?'

'Yeah,' said Jerra.

'Okay, start with A.'

Jerra looked up at him.

'A . . .'

'Come on.'

'Shit, nothin' starts with A.'

'What about amberjack?' said Sean, smiling.

'Yeah,' said Jerra, embarrassed as hell. 'Abalone?'

'Not a fish,' said Sean.

'Plenty of Bs. What about bastard-of-a-big-barramundi?'

The old man laughed.

They talked names for a while, wandering off the alphabet when cobia came up. Then it was just big fish.

'Nothin' else worth lookin' at, once you've seen a big fish. Thrashin' and jumpin' and thumpin' on the deck, spreading 'is gills like wings.' He watched Jerra nodding, 'Bloody sad business, too, seein' a big fish die. That's somethink else, boy. Ever seen it?'

'No,' he lied. 'I always clubbed 'em before they suffered. Didn't like to see 'em die.'

Hard silver and black, flat against the boards, laced with salty pearls, glistening. The gills lifting ponderously, straining, lifting, falling. A fingertip on the smooth eye. Short, guttural death-grunts. Tears of blood tracking the deck. The sleek silver of scales, sinews in the tail wearing to a feeble spasm. Every big one on the deck looked at him the same way as that turrum, dying open-eyed when they were ready. Jerra always left them there, stalling, his back to the other deckies.

'Strong lad, you must be.'

Jerra shrugged. The old man pulled on the stinking sea-slug of a smoke.

'Any deep stuff?'

'Not much further than the shelf. We used to pass the

whalechasers on their way in. Seagulls stuck to 'em like shit to a blanket.'

With the catch bubbling eyes and gills in the holds, tails flailing, mucous spittle raining, he would wait at the rail as Michaelmas Island came into view, and opening the sea with sneezing jets the porpoises would cut diagonally for the bows, waiting for cast-offs, running back on broad muscular tails, arching back in flourishing sweeps with open mouths, eyes entreating laughingly. Then they would catch up and wait for a whack from Jerra, taking turns at presenting their backs to the flat of the oar.

The morning he was thinking about other things, he hit too hard and the leader squealed. They never came again.

'Sometimes we'd take white pointers following the whales being towed in. Big as whales, too. Tearing great hunks of blubber out of the whales.'

'Catchin' them bastards is somethink.'

'Just as they came up on the gaff, I'd have to shoot. A couple of times. To be careful.'

Gaping, writhing in their own spray. Pink sheen. Thud-thud-thud of the tail against the stern. Gulls waiting.

'They're tricky buggers, orright. Mate o' mine, years back, lost a foot to a bronze. An hour out of the water it was. Red took to it with a cleaver.'

'You worked on the boats.'

'Oath. Did the salmon all along the coast. Sharks when it was bad. Small stuff, herring, snapper. We even went to abalone, one or two bad seasons.'

'Who's we?' asked Sean.

'Me an' the wife.' He dragged tea with sucking lips. 'How long you stayin'?'

'Got about three weeks,' said Jerra. Abalone. That's what his lips looked like; wet an' rubbery.

'Can't see anybody wantin' ter stay that long.'

'Pretty good here,' said Sean.

'Lots better places,' said the old man.

'Good coast,' said Jerra.

'Little bus, eh? All set up.'

Jerra nodded.

'Move around a bit yourself?'

'Not for years. Been to Perth. Bad times we drove up and sold straight to the rest'rants. Rabbitin' for a spell. Got away quick, though.'

'Didn't go much on it?'

'Too many big mouths. Bigger'n nor'west blowies.'

'What about smaller places around here? Albany, Ongerup?'

'All the same. Wherever there's a pub an' people to jabber they just go the same.'

'Albany's orright,' said Jerra.

'Yeah?' said the old man. 'What's it like there now?'

'Always seemed the same to me.'

'Probably too young to know it any different.'

'I s'pose so.'

'Bugger of a place, I reckon. Sailors' town. Yanks and Wogs walkin' round with the local girls. Make yer sick.'

Jerra nodded politely. He had friends in Albany once. Most of them had either gone to the city, were in gaol for dope, or had died driving big cars.

Smooth stones clicked. Bitter smoke mingled with the steamy breath of coals. Sean yawned, rubbing salt and smoke from his eyes.

'Fire's out.'

'Better let youse lads get some sleep.'

'Haven't finished your tea,' said Jerra.

'Gone cold, anyway.' He rose stiffly.

Nodding, the old man went slowly up the track, wrinkled khakis merging in the green-black night. Only the single red eye of his cigarette winked. That soon faded too.

sea-junk and
amberjack

Mornings. Afternoons. It was pointless counting. How could you count the warbles in the grey, colours in the fires, thuds in the bush, keep record of the morse of cicadas, seeds, sap, stems? Fish-bones burnt to a white powder, and scales clung to bark and licks of grass. Feet burred, nails caught, faces rimed with salt and smoke and dirt.

They cruised on the surface, listening to the breath in the snorkels. Jerra clamped on the rubber bit, feeling the goose-flesh creep along his arms, and saw a long slit at the crest of a hump of rocks and weed that crouched on the bottom. Sean dived across at a small goatfish, away from it. Jerra hovered. He kicked and sank into the weediness of the hole, pulling down the rubber. Prongs glinted. A twilight. Down. He cleared his ears, and the space widened as he kicked. Blennies and pomfrets poked their heads from fissures. His lungs pushed against his chest as he settled on the silt. Corroded things lay half-buried, twisted formations knotted on each other, furred with algal turf, as if the hole had collected the debris of many storms. He peered along wrinkles and ledges. Morwong shot, with lips of congealed blood, from hole to hole, and specks of light showed through the walls. There were other entrances, fresh currents on the bottom fed from somewhere back in the darkness that went further than he dared to go. His mask distorted: the walls seemed to curve. Breath short, he turned for the bar of light. And froze. Pugnacious jaws opened at him, peg-like teeth phosphorescent behind the blue lips. The pectoral fins quivered, balancing. It was as big as him.

He kicked upwards, hard, pulling at the water, making for the fluorescent bar, then through, into the silver, crashing the surface, gasping the warm air.

Sean surfaced.

'God, I though you'd gone for good!'

Jerra floated onto his back, pushing the mask back.

'Thought you must've drowned or something. Didn't even see you go in.'

Jerra spat the blood that came to the back of his throat.

Dripping gobs of butter, the fillets were sweet and firm. The white flesh broke off in their fingers.

'Lots of fish,' said Jerra. 'Sea-junk.'

'How deep?'

'About thirty.'

'How could you tell?'

'Ears.'

'Risky.'

Jerra did his best to ignore him. He was thinking.

On his back, Jerra drifted in and out. Sean read a hard-covered book. Jerra opened his eyes. His hair felt like unravelled hemp.

'Buggered if I can sleep.'

'Hmm.'

'What you reading?'

'Shit.'

'Catchy title.'

'Hmm.' He flicked a page. 'Seen Ben Gun since his midnight meeting?'

'Who?'

'The Old Man and the Sea. The wino from up on the hill.'

'Oh, him.' Jerra got up on an arm. 'How do you know he's a wino?'

'Did you see his face? Weathering the years, and more. The more is the piss. He's as mad as a cut snake.'

'Seemed orright to me.'

''Cause he talked about fish.'

'Held a conversation.'

'Flittin' amongst the tombs.'

'Got him sewn up, haven't you?'

'You saw him.'

'You're a bloody cynic.'

'Try it.'

'Must get a prescription.'

Sean went back to the book, smiling as he recognised one of his own lines. Jerra lay back.

'You must admit, though, he did look pretty wild. The shirt held together with nappy pins, the gummy smile.'

'Wonder where his wife is.' So many things were bothering him.

'Probably dreamt it up.'

'He was dinkum.'

'Got you fooled.'

'Least I didn't make an arse of meself.'

'Who says you didn't – amberjack.'

'I would've remembered.'

'He wouldn't know himself, probably.'

'He'd know a lot've things, I reckon.'

'You've been sucked, mate. Again.'

Eventually, they slept.

Into the soft dark before him, a silver gleam. Jerra sank in the blankets of eddying current. On the bottom, a blacker form, inside the skeleton. It sank darker, where he was hesitant. He longed to plunge into the thing, drag it thrashing into the clear, feeling the tough mosaic of scales, the muscle of tail, to brush lightly against the dorsals, to lever open the skull to see the pure white, feel it, hard as a pebble, in his palm. No breath. He clawed up the smooth curving walls for the surface, the clear sheen, feeling the grey coarseness against his cheek and neck, dry, chafing. In the smoke and gasps of kookaburras, his hands smelt of fish.

'Sean?'

'Yeah.' He rolled over.

'You remember the kinghie my old man caught on the jetty?'

'That was years ago.'

'I was eight.'

'What about it?'

'Remember the pearls?'

'Oh, you're not on that, again.'

'It happened.'

'You were eight years old; you imagine all sorts of bloody things, especially you. Gawd, between you an' your grandfather and . . .'

'It happened.'

'An' so there's these things inside a fish's head. It's all fishermen's bloody superstition.'

'Yeah.'

'Geez, Jerra. Next thing you'll tell me is that you know God and Father Christmas.'

'I've seen 'em.'

'Who, God and Father Christmas?'

'No, the pearls.'

'Arr.'

As an eight year old he remembered the noises the kingfish made as the air bladder deflated and the gush that came when his father opened it up and pulled out the roe, then opened the head and took one of the jewels from the base of the spine.

'Why don't you take them both, Dad? One for you an' one for me.'

'Leave one for the fish, eh?'

He did not understand, but his Dad knew. They put the pearl on the jetty next to the fishing bag, and took the fish down onto the lower landing to wash the guts out and throw the head away.

When they returned, the pearl had gone, slipped between the rough sleepers and disappeared into the dredged green.

all the men . . .

Mornings were cooler. Jerra walked along the beach, up and back in the arc, crossing and re-crossing tracks and prints, crab, bird, mud-skipper, man. His own tracks, hardened and smoothed, looked as though they might hold water if it rained. He spat into a baked footprint and the gob disappeared, even the little stain gone in a moment.

There was often new debris along the high watermark; globs of plastic, splinters of soft pine, bottles, a petrel without legs (this disturbed him greatly), lengths of nylon rope, sea slugs, abalone shells like pale, open hands, all tangled in the thin stain of weed which re-lined the brow of the beach. And lines in the sand half obliterated by the tide that could have been sand crabs, but there were hand marks, too.

Gulls would follow, hovering.

At a gilt dawn he found a seal under a wreath of birds. The eyes had gone. Flesh had perished and ruptured, peeling, burst upholstery. A green slit, the hollow belly opened to the sky. It was big, old. Some of the weedy whiskers still showed. Gulls snapped, and the stench, too, forced him back. Jerra could not take his eyes from the slit of belly. He wondered how long his mind could remain numb. He pretended that he was not pretending.

Sitting by the glowing mound spilling through the circle of rocks, Sean glanced up as he got back into camp.

'How's the swell?'

'Piss-poor.'

'Anything new?'

'A seal. Dead on the beach.'

'Goin' fishin'?'

'Yeah, some squid left.'

It was apathetic conversation, even for them.

Flakes of pollard dried on their hands. Lines bobbed on fingers. The squid dried in the sun, curling at the edges.

'Thought they'd bite this morning,' Jerra murmured.

Sean suggested seal meat, remembering Jerra's mention of the dead seal, but Jerra vetoed it quickly, stubbornly. If they were that desperate, he said, then he could dive and have a feed in ten minutes. It sounded arrogant, even to him, but it was true enough. He wasn't using the carcass of anything washed up to catch a fish.

Then Jerra had a hard bite that slashed the line down and across, wrenching his arm. A silver flash like a mirror.

'Skippy!'

He pulled hard, hand over hand, the beaded line coiling at his feet. The skippy came out, slapping and smacking the water. He held it against his leg, threaded the hook out, saw the trickle from the corner of its mouth, and tossed it into the bag.

'More of those, my son.'

It kicked in the bag.

'Bit of fight for a small fish,' said Jerra, wiping the papery scales onto his jeans.

'That's 'cause they swim sideways coming up.'

'Smart fish, skippy.'

'Trevally.'

'Not this side of the border.' Jerra cast again. He spread some pollard onto the water. 'What are you, a Sydney poonce?'

'Ho!' Sean dragged line. The fish slashed, skipped, shied, and was lifted onto the rock. 'Howzat, mate? Nearly a pound!'

Jerra meant to reply, but his line cut again. Down and across, then away, shivering. His hands burnt.

'He's turning, he's turning.'

It was bigger still, cold and sleek. The flanks were so fine, almost without scales. Sean laughed, slapping his side.

'They're bitin', mate!'

'That's the last of the squid,' said Jerra, threading it.

'Arr. Just when they were biting.'

'Oh well, there's enough for a feed.'

'What about seal meat?'

Back onto seal meat.

'Bugger off. You don't know what it's got in it. Been pecked over enough, anyway.'

Sun glared hot from the water. Sean sighed.

'What about the skippy? Why don't we cut a strip off one of those?'

He sliced the head off the biggest. It writhed in his hands. Blood ran on the rocks. He slit the belly and dug out the guts.

'What's this?'

Jerra leant over his shoulder.

'That? Worms.'

'Worms?'

'All through. Look.'

Sean threw it on the rock.

'You'd better try the others,' said Jerra.

'Ah, it couldn't be in all three.'

Jerra watched from the corner of his eye. The line shivered in the breeze. A gull screamed.

'All of them! Every bloody one!' Sean stabbed with the chipped blade. 'Oh, what a fucken waste.' He hurled the shabby things out onto the water.

They picked their way back through the rocks, pollard and scales clinging to their palms. Birds bickered on the water.

Sean strode ahead, muttering and looking up towards camp. Carrying the fishing bag, Jerra glanced down to the other end of the beach where he saw the tiny figure of the dog again. It got up on two legs and walked into the dunes.

Later in the day, after a depressing tinned lunch – pork and beans and a Big Sister self-saucing pud (cold) – Jerra went walking – for wood, he said to Sean who looked at him with curiosity – and he found himself heading back up the hill on the rutted track.

The grey ruts had smoothed in the afternoon winds. A rabbit scuttled across the track. The breeze blew his hair forward into his face. His hands smelt of fish. His jeans were crusty with pollard, sauce, blood, and scales.

Nothing was different. Only the crumbling footprints and drag marks from the jerrycan. Twenty-eights tittered in the movement of the trees.

Up at the shack, he stood for a while observing the silence until he found the courage to call out without unnerving himself.

'Hullo! You there?'

He tapped the door.

'Anyone there?'

He picked his way round the side, past the webs and rust of the tank, through the grass, flecked with hard old scales, past the brown and green bottles, until he was at the door again. Through cracks and knots in the shutters he could see a dim desolation, a fur of dust on the floor, broken glass in the corner, webbed, fluffed with dirt. Nothing lived here, he knew it.

As he trudged down the track, something thumped in the bush. A roo or perhaps a rabbit.

NO said the tree in scars and clots. He agreed, whatever it meant. NO sounded fair enough. Until you thought a bit.

He sat on the crest of a dune overlooking the crescent of the beach, the sun pummelling his back, and wondered about fishing. He wondered about the waiting his father said was so good. Dad's still waiting, he thought sadly. Geez, what'm I waiting for? To grow up?

He told himself to bugger off and started a poem, the sun on his back.

'All the men . . .' he said aloud, and nothing else came. 'All the men . . .' Stupid talking out loud, anyway. He gave up.

His grandfather was stuffed in the head thinking he would ever write poems. Jerra tried to remember the lines he had learnt but all he could remember was the deep mirror of water by the brewery and his little feet looking up at themselves.

Then he remembered Gran bringing cups of tea, all afternoon, tending Granpa's foot, hearing him whine, calling her out to the back yard.

Remembered his own feet looking up at themselves as he hung over the retaining wall by the brewery, trying to learn C.J. Dennis, and catch tailor on the scummy night tide of the Swan River.

He had forgotten the wood. He would get some tomorrow.

Sleep came slow. Sean breathed a metric rhythm. Dying fire flickered on the windows. Surf rumbled, coming, going. A cricket began, then faltered, started, stopped again. Jerra rolled onto his side.

N . . .	O . . .
no	oranges
not	old
needy	orientals
nok	off
neighbour's	oxen
Nag	O'Sarkey
nourishing	octopus
NOel	NOel
now	oracles

NO said the scar-faced tree, in his blackness of sleep.

Hovering. This wasn't waiting. He hesitated, plunged into its diamond side. It tore the spear from him. He went for the opening. It fled, jammed half-way, flexing, writhing, tearing. The water clouded. No breath, and the entrance was obscured.

Sean stirred, talking again.

The beach breathed deep.

fish and women
and bollocks

Bleached white as the sand, the beam wouldn't be moved. Whiskers of weed had caught in its coarsened grain. Bare white sticks, spindly crooked things, were all he could gather. Wind slopped the swell onto the shore. Sand was dredged up, swirled grey in the foam, almost settled, and was churned again as the shore ran with seething white.

Jerra sat on the beam, seeing the wind whip the bay. There was no real wood around. Not that he expected much. He gazed towards the granite tumble at the other end of the beach. In all his solitary walking, the bleary dawns when he felt cold inside and had to walk and convince himself that Sean knew nothing of his secret – he wouldn't be just cool and bitchy, he thought, he would be maniacal, tear him to ribbons – he had never ventured further than those blunt-faced boulders. He set off towards them, skirting the burst carcass of the seal that frightened him so much, triggering off all the memories. Close up, the rocks lost their darkness and smoothness and were blotched with little varices and pock marks, dissected by veins of algae, ribbed with salt. He climbed, walked carefully around the bigger boulders, and hopped to and from smaller ones. Nearer the surge, their surface was shiny and black, slick with turf, and in cracks and crevices running white with foam, beams, planks, and twisted white branches were wedged tight, old, old wood swollen and stuck hard in the rock.

Stumbling down the other side, he saw a crazily constructed

dwelling – a humpy of sorts – beyond the crisp high-water mark of a small cove beach. Dense brush, ferns, high timber and magpies crowded in on the little shack, hinting at a freshwater source, a spring, perhaps. The white hook of beach ran to more piled granite on a sheer fault-wall, toppling into the water. Gulls flitted across the cove, settling in the trees. Jerra whistled.

'Didn't expect to see you.'

Jerra spun. The old man.

'Frighten yer?'

'Yeah,' Jerra breathed. 'Again.'

'Lookin' for wood?'

'Right.'

'None 'ere. 'Cept for the hut. You can't 'ave that.' The old man wound his way down to the sand and sat at the base of a boulder, out of the wind. Jerra sat.

'Find anything?'

'Nah.'

'Haven't been up this end before?'

'Thought I'd come and have a look.'

'Caught any fish?' The old man didn't look up from rolling. The paper darkened as it slid along his tongue.

'A few skippy. Sweep, leatheries.'

'Fair enough.'

'The skippy had worms.'

He lit the end and Jerra watched it smoulder. It stank. The old man rubbed his scaly arms. Jerra carved in the sand.

'You said you lived in the shack up from us. Were you bullshitting?'

'Hmm.'

Jerra thought this over for a moment, waiting for the old man to explain, then, realising the old man had nothing to add, turned his attention to the humpy.

'Where'd you get the wood for the hut?'

'Driftwood, mainly. Found the tin on the other beach.'

'Must've taken ages.'

'I got plenty o' time.'

The ply walls shivered slightly in the wind, leaning in on themselves.

'Boat ply, isn't it?'

'Yeah.'

Smoke burnt Jerra's face, wafting over, a thin edge in his nostrils. Boat ply.

'Pretty rough, living out here alone.'

'Alone, yeah.'

'You like it, I s'pose?'

'Have to.'

'Lonely as hell.'

The smoke was shoved into the sand. A wisp seeped out, disappeared. The old man's belly strained against the safety-pins. When you looked closely at the sand, it was not really white, but a motley of gold and black. After a time, the black became dominant. Jerra blinked.

'See many people out here?'

'All that come.'

'Many come?'

'Enough.'

'When was the last?'

'Couldn't be sure.'

'Anyone been here before?'

'Not here. Not this beach. You're the first.'

'Always a first time.'

'Everything's been done. At least once.'

Both sat, eyes on the sand.

'You don't get on with him, do you?' The old man stated with authority.

'Yeah, sure I do.'

'Doesn't look like it.'

'How would you know?' He glanced quickly at the eyes behind the clotted beard.

'I met 'im. You remember, after a while.'

Jerra got to his feet, annoyed.

'Hey, who owns this land? The Crown?' Jerra was getting edgy about all this; he had enough on his mind already.

The old man smiled, taking out his stinging mixture to roll.

'It's mine. To the high water mark.'

'We're trespassers, then, eh?' Jerra lifted his chin. 'Didn't see any signs.'

The smile was bent.

'Well, didn't you now?' He rolled without looking. 'What's a sign? People shoot holes in it, knock it down.'

Jerra rubbed his thighs in agitation.

'They see you don't want 'em around, so they think they'll have a look. Wouldn't blink at the place, otherwise. Not lookin' for anything in particular.'

'Well – ' He thought of that damned tree, puzzled.

'Still, what people can't have is what they want most.'

'What the hell are you smoking?' Jerra asked in exasperation to change the flow of talk.

'Stinks?'

'Not baccy, is it?' It was impossible.

'Me mixture. Tea-leaves, seaweed, all sorts.'

'Stinks.' Jerra laughed. He sat again. 'Smells like the bollocks of Ben Cropp.'

'Ben Boyd, more like it.'

Then suddenly the old man was singing.

> *Well the south seas're fickle*
> *In the winters of June,*
> *An' the wind from the Pole sings the*
> *Riggin' a tune,*
> *When the sperm and the humpback*
> *Come northwards they say,*
> *When we found them in shallows*
> *Down at Two Peoples Bay, Two Peoples Bay.*

Jerra smiled, nervous.

'An old whaling song,' said the old man, sucking on his smoke. 'My ol' man taught me that. We 'ad whaling in the family, right back to Two Peoples Bay.'

'At Two Peoples?'

'That's where it started round here. Used to whale here when the bay whalers spread in the 1830s. Ten or fifteen blokes dropped on the beach with a keg of rum, a boiler, a boat and a gun. Used to row out to the whales that came in to sun and harpoon 'em, then wrestle one for a mornin' an' tow it back in. If they wasn't all towed out to sea. Next land south is the Pole. Bugger of a life, that. If the whales didn't get 'em, the Abos did, or they shot each other.'

'Now they use harpoon guns and spotter-planes and fast little chasers.'

'Not the same.'

'Yeah, I sup – '

The old man rattled off into the song again, mucus bubbling in his throat as he growled the swinging lines.

> Well we anchored her in and off old Coffin Island,
> A nor' wester blowin' the best of a gale,
> An' the beach was as white
> As a sweet vargin smilin' –
> The air around smellin', smellin' of whale.
> – smellin' of whale.

The old man smacked a hand on his thigh as he sang the chorus.

> Out in the longboats, then sailors.
> Put your backs to the oar.
> Mind a big bull don't come up an' nail us,
> Or we will be sailin' no more
> – We will be sailin' no more.

'Good song,' said Jerra when the old man didn't continue.

'Me an' the wife used to sing it.'

'Where's she?'

'On the other beach.'

'Eh?'

'She died. Burnt in the shed on the beach.'

'Shit. That's rough.'

'We used to argue a lot. She lived in the shed on the beach after a while.'

Jerra tasted it at the back of his throat.

'Some things you can't do anything about.' The old man fidgeted.

'Yeah, things go that way.'

'Yer just get the feeling of it all comin' down around you. Like sinking. Drowning.'

'Yes.' Yes! he thought.

'Like I said. What people want most. Always wanted to be a real man with the bollocks of Ben Boyd. Anyone's. I had to settle for the boat. That was the only time we were together, on the boat. It was orright then, with the boat. We wiped its bum like a kid. Still it was just a boat and not a kid. When she sank that there was nothin' left to hold her. So she thought, my lovely Annie. Gave her the pearl out of a kinghie's head, once. Beautiful. An' why do they throw it away an' want what you can't give 'em, eh? Eh?'

Then it was true. The pearl was true. He had heard nothing else. And he'd let it go, that time as a child in the boat, not letting it be cut up. A turrum should have one, his father said, but Jerra said no, seeing the eye staring again and the stricken mate diving at the moment of death.

'Why do they?'

'Not sure I follow you.' Jerra was thinking of fish; the old man was talking women and bollocks.

The old man got to his feet, disgusted.

Jewel. The name wouldn't go away. He couldn't always catch the face anymore. There were so many of them. A new face with each mood, each collapse, each mistake. But he wouldn't forget. Not if he could.

The seal had really irked him. He admitted it now, lying awake. Sean slept. Jerra was grateful. He doesn't look like her at all, he thought bitterly.

After a time, Jerra slept also. It was a trammelled sleep crowded with fish and women and bollocks.

little pieces came away every time he touched

Sun warmed their shiny black skins as they basked on the rocks. A clutter of gear surrounded them, glistening, the salt appearing as they dried, and below their feet, the glossy kelp rose and fell with the surge. They talked idly, drawling, deliciously drunk from sun and exertion. Jerra had been thinking about their growing apart. He knew it wasn't just the money and the intimidation. Deliberately, he turned the conversation towards women. It was a wilful thing. He wanted to prove himself right again. He mentioned Mandy Middleton.

'You remember Mandy. Course,' he said, eyes shut tight against the white of sun. Come on, you prick, he thought, tell me you don't.

'No. I don't.' Sean unzipped his wetsuit.

'You and Mandy were pretty close, weren't you?' he insisted.

'We got into a habit,' Sean sighed, irritated.

'She was a nice one, though. Gave you a good run.'

Sean snorted. 'A good run.'

'Always thought you'd get married, you know.'

Sean buzzed the zip up again, then down.

'You were, weren't you?'

'No.'

'Never did figure out why she left town in such a hurry. Always thought it would be you who pissed off.'

'Thanks.'

'You had your job to think about, though.'

39 𝒟

'Yeah.'

'She must've met someone bloody good.'

'Hmm?'

'She was off quick. Didn't seem any reason. Heard she was in Geraldton.'

'Who said?'

'Someone down the beach front. Ages ago. Phil. Said she was on her own.'

'Dumped, I s'pose.'

'In a nice motel.'

'That's good,' he said dully.

'Dunno how she can afford it.'

'Probably works. Some of us do.'

'Hope she comes down again, some time. She was good fun.'

'I don't think she'll come back.'

'No. Maybe not.' Bastards. Same as your old man. Just get rid of 'em to save embarrassment.

A crab tumbled across the rocks below. It skittered into a crack above the waterline. Jerra lay back, satisfied that he had confirmed it again. He smiled, perversely, bitterly. He almost enjoyed the hurt of knowing it was all over between them; it was only a matter of time. And, a second later, he wished it could be still the same as the old days. He cursed himself. It was all bloody stupid. God, we're all bloody stupid, he thought.

'Where'd you go yesterday?' asked Sean, rubbing the hairs on his chest.

'Up the beach.'

'See anything?'

'Driftwood.'

'Didn't bring it back.'

'Wedged into the rocks.'

'Lot of use in the rocks.'

'Got some mallee roots up the track this morning.' Always me getting the wood, he mused bitterly.

A leg reached from the dark, scorched red and orange. The claw flexed and retreated into darkness.

'Coming in again?' Jerra asked, feeling the hard teeth of the zip on his chest.

'I'll stay in the sun.'

Jerra clipped the weights on. His feet slipped into the flippers. One yellow, the other blue. Like thongs. Never a pair. Different brands, even.

'Why do you reckon I've got odd flippers?'

'You can't pick a pair.'

'They're a pair.'

'Not even the same size. No wonder you get fish. Curious to see what sort of dickhead they're up against.'

'Arr. Jealous.' He thumped Sean matily, and slid down to the water.

The crab skidded across the rock into darkness. The water was cool.

Leaning under, he slid down shallow and followed the bottom, the curving fall, as long as he could bear it, then surfaced, clearing his snorkel, and wandered along the surface. He pushed out past the big, incongruous hump towards the limits of the reef, wrinkled with trenches, channels, open pores of holes with weed sawing back and forth on itself, wallowing on the crags that sheltered schools of tiny pomfrets and bullseyes clouding silver and yellow in potholes. Green wrasse cruised the bottom for food.

Jerra watched from above, gliding, with a wrasse circling idly in the cover of his shadow. He ducked and slid down behind the fish, took out his knife and prised an abalone from the bottom. It sucked on his palm. He dropped it. The wrasse watched. He floated up. It circled the exposed meat. After a few moments, it nudged the shell and left.

In a long, steep trench, Jerra saw a clutch of queen snapper feeding near the bottom. He descended from behind, feeling the rubber bite into his thumb. The fish clung. Just as he chose a target, the leader turned side on. The others baulked, spreading blue, and Jerra lunged, catching the leader behind the gills. They struggled all the way to the surface, trailing a mist of blood. It was as big and blue as his left flipper, the yellow lines radiating from its eyes like wrinkles. He thrust it, threshing, into the bag, tore it from the barbs and dived.

The others had grouped further along the trench, about six of them, wary and slow. They fanned quickly, seeing the black shadow descending. Jerra chased one of the bigger fish to a pothole, weeded over and dark. He waited, his guts tight. The blue head appeared. Prongs pierced the forehead and gills. It was dead before Jerra had it on the surface.

The bag and his legs were heavy. He struck for the rocks. As he slopped the bags onto the rock, the first fish twitched.

'A couple of blues,' he said, nasally, the mask pinning his upper lip.

Sean looked up.

'Bit of quality for a change, eh?' He slipped them out, fingers in the gills, and laid them on the rock. 'Nice size, too. A few pound. Let's go back and have an early tea.'

'Nah,' said Jerra, spitting a pink gob onto the water. 'I'm going back for another look. Check 'em for worms first.'

He shivered. Always colder the second time. Worse the third. His white nails glowed against the blue of his fingertips. Tiny bubbles gathered on his knuckles. Shafts of light webbed the water. It was like swimming under a net. He tightened the weights.

He found the holes again, in the odd-shaped hump in the reef.

It opened darkly, awash with trailing strands of black. He kicked down, tightening, and followed the clean silver of steel. His spear scraped the rock, leaving a welt. Sweep and morwong cluttered the shaft and fanned like red and black feathers as he approached. A crusted circle of barnacles lay in the silt. Ledges opened black on all sides, as he rolled to see them all, wondering why they were so even and well-formed, so precisely hewn by the sea. It was unnerving, this orderly cave.

– A porcelain globe faced him, solid as the head around it, encasing it. Scales fanning from the heavy gills, flat terraces fading into the distance of tail and cave. It watched him, monstrous, motionless, current drifting cold from behind. Jerra's palm met the soft bottom. The hard edge of something pressed into his thigh as he settled, aiming. The rubber of the handspear cut. He waited. Longer. The fish turned and bared its side, jowls twitching. Jerra aimed for the softness and the spine behind the gills. It was gone into the dark.

He turned to surface. Rust chafed his leg. He pulled at the curious formation. It peeled from the barnacled bed of its own imprint and he held it against his side, uncovering rotten wood as he found a handhold, aghast as well as almost black from exertion. Timber gave way beneath his heels as he rammed up.

Sean was gone. Jerra slid up onto the flat rock. The fish were still in the bag, floating in a rock pool. He chased an orange crab from the pool. A corner had been chewed out of the bag, but the fish were untouched.

'That's right, leave me to clean the bloody fish.'

Knots of guts fell onto the rock. The gulls hung, cackling. He washed the clean, firm, curving fillets, and kicked the offal into the pool that was scummed at one edge with a skin of larvae. Flies walked on the water's skin.

'Get it while you can, crab, you crazy ol' bastard.'

Jerra threw his gear into the big sack with Sean's, put the rusty circle in, and tossed the lot over his shoulder. It was coarse on his back.

'Some cave. Reckon we're both crazy.'

The crab clattered.

The old man eyed Jerra, pools quivering in his eyes.

'Whatcher got there?'

'Ringbolt. Isn't it?'

'Could be.'

Birds were fidgeting in the ashy sand.

'It's a ringbolt for sure.'

'Hard to tell.' Keeping distance. 'There's no bolt left, nothin' to attach it to anything.'

'Worn away. Yours, isn't it?'

'Could be.'

'It is. I know.'

'You don't.'

'Don't you want it?' Jerra offered. The old man retreated.

'What for?'

'Dunno. Thought you might like to keep it.'

'You keep it.'

'You should.'

'I said I don't want the bloody thing!' The old man snatched it from him and held it over his head, as if to fling it into the water. He dropped it at Jerra's feet and walked away.

It was a crusty, eaten thing in Jerra's hand as he climbed back. It left stains on his hands. Little pieces came away every time he touched.

The day after, Jerra went back to the clinker-built fossil in the reef and found that there were crays nestling in its hoary beams which he had previously overlooked, and he brought one of them – the biggest, like an armoured car – back to camp where Sean had spent the day reading *The Rise and Fall of the Third Reich*. Sean, he had to admit, was impressed.

'Two pounds if it's an ounce.'

'Metric now, mate,' he said, happy for a moment.

'Same in metres.' Sean laughed. 'How long since we had one o' these?'

'Dongara.'

'When you speared that ray.'

'We all have our moments.'

Jerra propped the bucket in the flames, chuckling at the memory of Sean being towed along the bottom by the startled foot-mat of a ray.

'Were there any more?'

'A few.'

'Should have got them.'

'Yeah.'

The water stirred, clusters of bubbles at the edges. Sticks and flames bone-cracked. It boiled.

'Put 'em in.' Jerra got up.

'Where you going?'

'The annexe. Gonna tidy up.' The rattle of limbs thrashing. Flesh. Boiling. He closed the flap.

A verse almost came to him in his half-sleep. He held his breath while it fumbled around inside him . . . *all dressed in clobber white* . . . *An' as their snowy forms go steppin' by* . . . Something, something. It escaped him.

Pickets, tickets, wickets. Crickets: the clicking tongues of a drumful of crabs, each their own clock, ticking. The smell of crayfish twitched in the blankets. He opened his eyes.

'Funny we never saw any of those crays before,' said Sean with his chin on the pillow. He had been shaving. Orange and yellow firelight flickered on the window.

'They were hidden away.'

'Odd colour.'

'They're called golddiggers. A southern cray.'

'Strange so close in.'

Jerra had a few ideas why they were so close in. Like the boat being loaded with a catch when it went down.

'How come you're not diving?' he asked Sean.

'Oh, it gets a bit silly after a while. Swimming in circles.'

'Thought you liked it. You were crazy on it, once.'

'Oh, it's the same stuff.'

'You always see something different. It's never the same.'

'Who wants to swim in circles the rest of their life?'

The moon was a pale fillet. Jerra saw it in the hairs on his arm. Sean's eyes were pink, blinking.

'Ever thought about diving to the bottom more often? In the caves. Always different. Another world.'

'Taking it a bit seriously, aren't you?'

'What do you take seriously any more?'

'There's other things in the world.'

'Yeah?'

'Fish! It's not the only bloody thing there is.'

'Oh yeah?'

'For you, maybe, and your father, and the crazy ol' bastard up the hill, but not me.'

'We don't appreciate the *better* things, I know.'

'Arr.' Sean laughed.

'None of which you could think of for the shares in yer head an' the shit in yer heart. What are you now?'

'Talking like a loony!'

'Everyone's a fucken *loony*. A loony. Someone that doesn't suck the crap is a loony. You learned orright. You got taught well, mate.'

'So? You learnt fish. Ah, yes.'

'An' you ate 'em. You lived it. It was the only family you had, mate – ours! Where was yours! Flittin' around EU–rope havin' a good time!'

'Fish! Fish! Shit!'

'Didn't hear you complain. Ever.'

'Yer too obsessed to hear.'

'That what you told yer old lady? Never gave her a bloody moment. Oh, yeah, she was a bloody first-class loony.'

Sean laughed hard. 'And a bloody idiot, Jerra. Like you.'

Jerra shifted back, pulling even breaths. Then he knew that Sean didn't know about him and her. That would have been the moment of a lifetime, an opportunity Sean would not have missed if he had known and been waiting.

'You talk in your sleep, you know.'

'So what.'

'Oh – '

'Come on.'

'You called for your mother.' He waited one second. '"Mum", you said.'

'Get fucked, Jerra,' said Sean quietly. 'Just get fucked.'

Jerra pulled the blanket up. It was hot and the blanket itched where he sweated. His face itched with triumph and shame.

'Sean doesn't love his Mum.'

'Yes, he does.'

'Has he ever said it?'

'Nah, boys don't say it.'

'I've heard you say it.'

'Well, I'm a bit strange, 'cause I hang around with you.'

'Yes, I'll bet,' said Auntie Jewel, sipping her lemonade that smelled funny, looking out over the quay.

In his dream in the half-stern shuddered with all the fish in the ocean, living in the skeleton that had grown a skin again. He swam off the edge, looking for the cutting edge of bow. It was blue for ever; he blacked without reaching bottom.

Walking, next morning.

A glimpse only, but he was sure. The tree grew an arm which disappeared suddenly. A crackle of leaves, the outline at the crest of the dune. Enough to give you the creeps. The ragged shirt was unmistakable.

All morning Jerra walked the same arc of beach, guiltily picking over the weed, uncovering tiny new things, textures, smells. He felt the corrugated skin of a shell, different shades of white and black in the sand, the minuscule air holes left in the wet sand by the sand crabs that came out and ruttled around in the dark with their run-stop-run-stop movements, and disappeared in the day, buried in the wet sand of the shore.

He tried his poem again. He'd call it 'NO', just to satisfy the tree.

NO
All the men . . .

All the stuffed men? 'Stuffed' was no good; not poetical enough. 'Pushed'? 'Cut'? He thought of whaling and fishing for a moment, and the old man's song that he couldn't really remember. Bollocks. Bollocks to the rowlocks. That's how he felt: balls to the wall. He tried the poem again.

NO
All the severed men.

As Jerra turned again to walk back, the old man tumbled down the dune at the end of the beach. Jerra could hear the rattly breath.

'Son! Son! Aren't you gonna come back home an' see yer Mum? She'll be pleased, orright. Geez, you've grown. "Born of . . . fire," eh.'

'What?'

He really stank this time. His hands were filthy, covered in heavy black flies.

'She'll take me back, she'll forgive me, no one will laugh, she'll love – '

Jerra stood back. The old man was peering into his face, but the eyes weren't there. Focused elsewhere. He stomped, moving around and back, slapping his thighs.

'You orright?'

'They'llcomesoonif yerdon't comeandseeer she'llbe surprised we'llbe altogetherbutwegottahurry!' The eyes were gone. There were pieces of bark in his beard.

'Who's coming?' Jerra laughed. 'Must be a gala thing every time somebody turns up.'

'Nnono! Yerdoanunnerstan! Sheelbringitallback, floatitagain!'

'Who? Float it? Who?'

'Quick, quick.'

Jerra kicked at the shells and the little air holes. The old man was hobbling up the dune after somebody else. Jerra had his own problems.

'Alistair MacLean?' Sean asked, smiling dryly.

'So?'

'Shit.'

'Thought you'd like him.'

'Alistair Mac-bloody-cLean?'

'Makes millions.'

In a tree this time. Sleeping in a tree, wedged in the fork beneath the umbrella of twigs and leaves. He decided not to go close. The old sod might fall, he thought.

'I just can't understand it.'

They argued about Alistair MacLean again.

'Arr, not again.'

'Same plots shuffled differently each time.'

' . . . '

'Same faces.'

Jerra drew joining triangles in the dust on the roof. A diamond. Grains settled on the blanket.

'Nothing changes. It doesn't get any better – or worse.'

'Just talked yourself up yer own arsehole!'

'Bullshit. How?'

'What's history? You read *that*, and stay awake a lot of the time. Don't talk to me about repetition!'

Sean fell back on the pillow. Jerra switched the yellow light out. Probably was crap, he thought, but you had to say something. Anyway, he'd seen repetition, *and* the bastards had gotten away with it, like father like son.

. . . A tart I knoo a 'undred years ago . . .

He knew that line.

Next day, he dived in the bowels of the wreck.

He came up with a writhing cray in each hand, heavy tails punching water. Near the surface he let them go. They spidered down, straight for the slit, disappearing into the black, feelers last. It was too much like grave-robbing.

Late in the afternoon, he went in search of the old man; he needed to talk, and probably to listen. The humpy was empty, showing no sign of being slept in for a while. The coals were old. Jerra saw the magazine pictures – *National Geographic* – stuck on the walls, yellow, ragged things with touched up teeth and gums.

The bunk had blankets. A tin full of whale oil stood on a box in the corner, and bent hooks, knots and twists of nylon and gut hung from nails in the beams which held back the ply walls, which, in turn, were clawed by weeds from the outside and grizzled with the skeletons of mussels and barnacular flakes like so many scales. A sliver of mirror stood against the windowsill, half obscuring a brown curlicue of lace; it cast a blade of light onto the Perspex window. The window, distorted only slightly, was caked with fat and fingerprints.

Out on the little beach, gulls huddled white in the sand. Jerra sat on the mouldy bunk and picked up the empty spine of a Bible, the cover of which was soft and green with mildew, with the blue vein of a marker still intact. Inside, catching on the seam of the binding, were a few tiny slips of paper, fragments cut crookedly which Jerra smoothed with a thumb.

> *– innocent blood –*
> *– the guilt of –*
> *– in your land –*
> *– careful –*
> *– cities of refuge –*

Jerra turned them over. Only half-words on the back. He closed the empty spine, thoughtful, and put it back on the floor. What floor there was to the place was deckboards, he knew. A shattered, watermarked compass, big as a head, stood on a crate by the bed. The fireplace was a cairn of limestone poking through the roof where splinters of light pierced the warped, black tin.

He waited. The old man did not come.

'I came over yesterday,' said Jerra, unbending the wire.

'I know.'

'Where were you?'

'Around. What's that?'

'Wire. I found it on the beach. Thought you might want it.'

'What for?'

'The loose tin.'

'Yeah.'

'It'll leak, this winter.'

'Yeah. I'll caulk it up, somehow.'

Jerra tossed it next to the old man. It coiled again, how he found it.

'Why didn't you want your ringbolt?'

'How would you like livin' with a corpse?'

'Eh?'

'Look, son, you know what I've done. They'll come out an' get me sooner or later. You can't do somethin' like that an' expect to get away with it.'

'Your wife?'

'Confessed a million bloody times, but no one's ever heard it. Heard nothin'. The screams, the boards crumblin' and the roof groanin'. . . . but I'm not gonna just let 'em take me. Orready done me time, I 'ave. I got burnt, too, you know. Standin' there all night. Pouring diesel on. Just white an' black when the sun come up, again. Smell of diesel, clothes . . . can't give 'em what they want most . . . they ruin what yer have . . . that boat was our marriage. Only thing bindin' us. Then you ruin what's left once yer alone with yer conscience. So. I've said it.' He laughed and bit the heel of his thumb.

Jerra would have spat.

'Well, I'm not going to tell anyone. I promise.'

'Arr.'

'Bloody beans,' muttered Sean. He tore the label off and put the can in the flames.

'Eatin' like the poorer classes, eh?' Jerra said pointlessly.

'Like eating rabbit shit.'

A crash in the bush.

'Close,' said Sean.

'Should've brought the .22.'

'Even beans are better than roo.'

Jerra poked the can with a stick. The fire was feeble.

'I'm thinking of leaving soon.'

'What? There's a week left.'

'Yeah. Well I thought we might move on.'

Sean was shaking his head, red eyes laughing.

'In the morning.'

'Shit, why not tonight?'

'Plenty of other places.'

'The old man of course. Geez. I don't *believe* it.'

'You know how ol' blokes like that are.'

'Yeah. But do you?'

The fire smouldered, smoke easing from between the teeth of coals. Sean dragged the black can from the ashes.

'Doesn't look like it's gonna get any hotter without wood,' he said, rolling it in the damp leaves at his feet.

'If you want some wood, there's plenty o' bush,' Jerra said. 'If yer not sure, the dead stuff usually burns best. You'll probably find it lying on the ground.'

Sean slapped beans onto the buckled plates.

'Here, smart-arse. Mind the bones.'

Sean was calling, asleep in the VW. Jerra couldn't stand it. He felt like going in there and throttling him. He sat by the circle of blackened rocks, scraping the soot away with a stick. The limestone showed dull white, bone, beneath. Dew settled on the back of his neck. No wind. Not a leaf moved.

He left the fire. It was too late to bother about more wood. He stumbled down to the beach in the moonlight. The white flickered through the trees. The sand was loud. Footsteps crunched, the broken teeth of shells. Walking near the still shore, he saw the buried beam, longer and whiter in the moonlight.

Difficult on the rocks. Shadows made it impossible to judge blackness as solid rock or air, and he fell a few times, opening an elbow and a shin. Feeling his way over the surfaces with his palms, he came upon the gulls, crowded, sleeping in a hollow. He avoided them, climbing closer to the water, slipping on the damp felt of algae.

Orange and red, the fire lit a circle in front of the humpy, rippling shadows across the sand, lighting the eyes of the old man, squatting, staring in.

He was cutting with little scissors, a pair of women's nail scissors.

. . . neighbours' landmark, which the men . . . of old have set. Fifteen: A single . . . wit . . . ness shall not prevail against –

Rolling, rolling the stuff between his fingers.

. . . or see this great fire any more, lest I die . . .

Jerra jumped from the last rock.

. . . And the rest shall hear, and fear, and shall never again commit any such evil among . . .

The old man, without a shirt, stood up and backed away.

'No, not me. Go away. I had to!'

Jerra stopped.

'No, hang on, it's me.'

The old man hobbled into the darkness of the humpy.

'Not all my fault. Don't, no burning. Please!'

'Hey, it's only me. It's orright,' called Jerra, going over to the hut.

'She sank it on purpose, you know. She ever tell you that? Did you ever . . . were you ever with her? Eh? Must've been the only one left in town, then. Was it yours? What she had in her? Not mine, oh no. Couldn't've. Not that she'd know. *A single witness . . . go away.*'

'I am,' said Jerra, annoyed. 'Tomorrow.'

'No. Go now. I loved, that's somethin'.'

'Yeah.'

'Been waiting, you know. Hard to find, eh? Have to get me twice if yer countin'. *Two!*'

'I could meet you up at the shack, tomorrow.'

A confused muttering from the darkness. Short laughs. Something scraped on the floor. A piece of wood fell in the sand next to Jerra.

'I've 'eard yers talkin' about me in me dreams . . . *send* n' *fetch him* . . . an' *fetch* . . . can't drag me down there to burn. Arr, yer bastards!'

Climbing the rocks, Jerra could hear the hollering, a flat echo off the rocks.

The VW hawked, then started with the old clatter, and the exhaust blew dust and scales from the grass behind. Sean slopped some water on the windscreen and got in, slamming the door. It fell open again. He cursed, slammed it again.

Jerra turned in the clearing. He gazed a moment at the windblown beach and the cairn of blackened stones.

Rain had hardened the sand. It was darker and packed in the ruts.

'Anti-bloody-climax,' murmured Sean, against the window.

'Veedub's mine. We all have our moments of power.' He slid into the bends, frightening birds into the air, and the shack came into view. Jerra pulled over.

'The last farewell,' Sean sneered, glancing at Jerra's grazed elbow.

Jerra went over to the hut and hit the wall. He thought the old man might have come up to say goodbye.

'You there?' Bubbling of the VW. 'It's me.'

'Might've slipped to the other side. You know, psychically.'

'Pass some paper.' Holding the paper against the window. 'Ah. Hadn't thought – '

'Hmm?'

'His name. Can hardly write anything if I don't know his name.'

'Jekyll?'

'For shit's sake!'

'Seen it all before. Movie, perhaps.'

'Bugger it,' said Jerra, climbing in and slamming the door. He yanked the handbrake. 'Let's just go; that'll be enough.'

He gave it a little. And missed second with a crunch.

PART TWO

what you'd
want most

Sudden cold days of autumn. Jerra felt the dull hardness of the bedroom walls as he overlooked the prim tablecloth of the garden next door, its zig-zagged edges, hemstitched borders with bougainvillaea and little drooping mauve things that clung tight; seeing the same things that had excited him in those early years when it was like living in a tree-house looming above the silky oaks, being higher, even, than the jacaranda clouds that were now an old, hard purple, and thick enough, it seemed, to walk on. The two storey house in Nedlands had been an abrupt change, he remembered dimly, from the weatherboard place at North Beach. Night times, when he couldn't sleep, Jerra would lie listening to the tide coming in at Cottesloe; it was six miles away, his father said, but he could hear it, anyway. Now all he heard was the traffic on Stirling Highway and the long breath of the downstairs air conditioner.

Sunlight was a neat square on the shag. There were books and photographs on the shelves, dents in the wall from bats and balls, and, above his pillow, a small footprint that wouldn't come off.

Under the silky oak the downy leaves were the same, crackling beneath his feet, wet in the coarse chill of the mornings. Early, the man next door tortured the mower into life and chased it around until lunchtime, shouting when the soft cores of dog turds bit into his shins.

Jerra was watering the nature strip, which didn't need it.

'Son.' His father nodded, hands in the pockets of his loose grey trousers.

''Lo, Dad.' The water was numbing his fingers.

His father sniffed, staring at the kangaroo-paw.

'Been thinking much?'

'About what?'

'What you're gonna do with yourself. Long time since you had work.'

'Yeah, I know.'

'Though you might've stuck at the boats longer. I thought you liked fish.'

'I do.'

'Better still, you liked catching the buggers. Not often you'd be disappointed on the boats. Caught a pile. Or you said so in your letters.'

'It's not the same.' He was spraying the pickets of the fence, long lashes on the rough boards, for the sake of the kangaroo-paw. 'It's the skill. Learnt that, if nothin' else. Like you used to say, the touches on the line, or like divin' for 'em on their own terms, not hauling them in by the ton with a winch. That's like . . . mining, or something.'

He heard the quiet breathing over the spray of the hose. A dog cleared its throat.

'Yeah. Not the same. But you can't expect – '

'Sure, nothing's all roses. But it's just not right. Nothing seems to be right.'

'When I was your age – '

'Dad – '

'Orright, just listen. Younger than you, I was, and your grandmother came home one day, pulled me in by the ear, and said – '

'"Yer an apprentice boiler maker", I know.'

'And that was it.'

'Easy.'

'No choice.'

'And no big decision.'

'It's never just one decision. But I went.'

'But time – '

'Seven years.'

'Then what?'

'I shot through.'

'Convincing me of the wrong side, Dad.'

'But you got a choice.'

Jerra stamped his feet.

'I ended up doin' a million things.'

'Ever happy?'

'Sometimes. There's always something else.'

'Then, there was. This is now. It's different.'

'Maybe.'

'Be easier if I had something to inherit.' Jerra grinned. 'Then I could just take over when you went dribbly.'

'Sean?'

'Yeah. No problems, eh?'

'No choice, either.'

'Choice is nothin' when there's zero to choose from. A shop with one product. That's choice?'

His father kicked the grass.

'Take it away, and that's what you'd want most.'

'Well, what made you settle down?'

'Dunno,' said his father. 'Got tired, I s'pose.'

'Not satisfaction?'

'Maybe that's one o' the things you stop worryin' about.'

'Where does that leave *me*, then?'

'Maybe you'll find something. I thought you might finish Uni, like young Sean, and get qualifications.'

'And end up like him? A degree to be a clerk for his old man. In a shirt business? Working out the pay and the collar measurements. What a life!'

'He could've got a job elsewhere.'

'Dad, BAs aren't worth a piss in the river these days.'

His father turned off the hose. It went limp and Jerra threw it down. The pickets shone.

'I don't care what you do, as long as you find something you can be satisfied with.'

'Take me till I die.'

'I thought that once.'

Jerra looked at the greying man, the loose skin around his neck, the pitted palms he remembered gloved in pollard.

'Not the same,' he said, certain.

'I'm not so sure.'

City streets were cold in the mornings where Jerra wandered, squinting into shopfronts, sitting with the hung-over drunks and the picking birds in Forrest Place, walking mornings without recall, looking dully into the brown froth of the river, over the shoulders of bent old men who fumbled with empty hooks, muttering. They spat on the water, the gobs floating out in the viscous current, like jellyfish. He might have spoken to them, but they just looked over their shoulders, as if to accuse him of scaring the fish away. He could have told them that there were none left, only their jellyfish. They muttered, and cricked their knuckles.

Jerra met eyes he knew, letting them blink by, clacking up the footpaths amidst the stink of rotting flowers, fluorescent windows of scaled, headless fish, the chatter of money in tills, on bars, in pockets, gutters.

Faces in the street had that grin. That tight sucking back of the lips. He was grinning, aching. His father was grinning, hand tight on the throttle. And the turrum was dying. In murmurs. But he had worked hard for it. He ached. Wasn't that enough?

He caught the grass-green bus home. Next door, the man was scraping up the turds with a shovel. A disgrace, it was, and he didn't even own a dog! Jerra grinned, ran his hand along the sucked-in cheek of the dented VW, and went inside, his clothes reeking of cashews from Coles, the newsprint and cement.

'Books,' his mother murmured, smoothing the wrinkles of his bed. 'Always used to have your beak in a book. Ever since I can remember. *Robinson Crusoe*, *The Swiss Family Robinson*, that little

skinny book you read at school . . . here, *The Old Man and the Sea*.
A writer, you said, that's what, Mum. And you'n Auntie Jewel
would sit out there in the afternoons, planning your career.
Scribbling those little poems. Didn't know who was worse, you
or Jewel. Those funny little love things she used to write. She was
a dear.'

Petals fall like scales onto my hand . . .

Jerra half-smiled, feeling the wall.
  'You used to read everything, once. News, pamphlets, maga-
zines. Even the *Digest*.'
  'Yes.' He smiled truly. 'Even the *Digest*.'
  'Why is it you don't read any more, Jem? The hardbacks, all
the old writers. What about Laurie . . . Laurie, no Lowry, the
drunken bum.' She found *Lunar Caustic* on his shelf and worried
it out. 'That's him.'
  'Dunno, Mum.' Jerra didn't look. The books turned him cold.
'It just wasn't real. You kid yerself, sometimes.'
  'You used to say it was more real than anything.' She shrugged,
pulling at her cardigan. She gazed at the curling photos, dusty on
the wall, and pointed. 'Where was that again, love?'
  'Near Esperance. I forget.'
  'Lovely.'
  'Yeah. It was.'
  'Who took the picture?'
  'Sean. Sean did. He had the camera.'
He glanced out onto the street.
  'Haven't seen our Sean for a while.'
Sprinklers rattled.
  'Have you seen him since the trip?'
  'No,' he lied.

Coming back from the river, he had gone into a bar. Lunch time,
and it was crowded with smoke and the smells of powdered bodies
swirling in the crush. Office girls laughed. A race-caller jabbered.

61 🖊

He bought a beer and found a red table with Vinyl seats. As he nudged the bitter foam, Sean came in, hesitated, then recovered and sat down.

'G'day, mate,' he said cheerily.

'Hullo, Sean.'

'How's things?' He flicked back his tie. The name tag looked impressive and a bit pathetic.

'Orright.' Jerra pushed a soggy coaster.

'Got a job, yet?'

'Nah.' He smiled. 'How's the shirts?'

'Well as can be expected, I s'pose. Which reminds me, I'm due back.' He stood, leaving a handmark on the hot red of the Laminex. 'Listen, I'll drop by soon and we'll go out somewhere on a weekend, orright?'

'Yeah, sure,' Jerra said into his beer.

Then only the smoke and the races. And the beer was awful.

' . . . can always remember it. Auntie Jewel would never have forgiven me for sending him there. Such a rough mob at that school.'

'Eh?'

'Auntie Jewel.'

'Talk about being sent.'

'Well, Sean's Dad thought it was for the best.'

'His best. Runs in the blood.'

Through sand.

'Everything's alright between you and Sean, isn't it, Jem? Nothing happened while you were away?'

'Nothing.'

'Hmm?'

'Ah, it's okay, I suppose. We just . . . '

'What?' She picked a piece of fluff from his jumper.

'Oh, I dunno. It's not the same, any more.'

'Oh, Jerra, what happened?'

'*Nothing*. Hard to explain.'

She ran a palm along the shelves.

'All those years. Since you were babies.'

'Yeah, I know.'

She sucked her top lip.

'Wasn't it a good trip? You did come home early.'

'Oh, it gets to the point where it's a bit of a drag. Seems you spend all your time sitting round keepin' the fire going.'

'I'd better get tea on.'

He lay back on the bed.

'Don' think it's all me. You don't know him any more, Mum. I don't either.' Or maybe I do, he thought. Only too well.

'Jerra.'

'All those years, his old man prancing around, droppin' her in hospital every time they slipped up. Having *him* here, like an adopted son, or something. Sean doesn't give a turd. You raised somebody who doesn't wanna remember. We're dirt!'

'I'm going downstairs for the tea.'

'Downstairs! I wish you'd sell this place, if it was ever bought. We don't belong here.'

'You speak for yourself. Your father and I do.'

''Cause you were weak? Or was it more complicated than that? It stinks. Maybe we are a bit dirty? It makes yer feel grubby.'

'What rubbish you talk!' His mother blinked. 'All this lying around has softened your head. Come down and peel the potatoes.'

'There's things you haven't told me, isn't there?'

'Jerra, of course not!'

'Is it about this house?'

'Don't even know what you're talking about.'

'No, neither do I.'

'That's not a bad poem,' he said.

'A bit soppy?'

'Only a bit. The sand bit's good.'

He mouthed the words, and she stretched in the sun.

'The sand bit, yes,' Auntie Jewel whispered.

The day he came home from the beach, after the police and the ferrety reporters.

'Sean, she's dead.'

'Yeah.' Sean closed the door of his bedroom in Jerra's face.

Falling against the wall, sick with it, Jerra cried out.

'You called for your mother.'

'Get fucked, Jerra. Just get fucked.'

'You're a bastard! Sean! You don't bloody care!'

Laughing. Behind the door. Jerra wanted to see his face.

'So she's dead.'

My love seeps like water through sand . . .

Buried alive.

Papers and cans rolled along the tacky bitumen. Seagulls scrabbled over a pizza, picking at the vomitty stuff, pulling it out of each other's beaks. Goatee-ed surfers were sitting on the bonnets of their vans. Boards piled up on racks, bright, glossy. A paunchy man with a metal detector combed the sand, stooping, straining it through his fingers.

There was a hole punched in the bin next to Jerra. Around the rusty puncture was scratched:

a r s e h O l e

Salt crusted the cyclone wire of the fences. People were leaning, talking, brushing the bleached hair from their eyes.

'I s'pose they told you about last night,' said the old lady on the bench next to him. She was chewing, chewing. There was nothing in her mouth, not even her teeth. She chewed a bit more.

'No.' Jerra put his feet up on the fence in front. He watched the swell breaking through the diamond pattern of the wire.

'Young people. Don't know what to do with themselves.'

He knew she was including him. He had the hair.

'Yeah.'

'That young boy. In the telephone box.'

'What did he do?' He felt he had to ask.

'Went crazy. Kept sayin' things. That they'd done to him. That no one would help him. Kept yellin' out, "Listen, – listenlistenlisten – "'

'Then what?'

'Blew his own head off. In the telephone box, over there.'

'God – '

'If someone don't put 'em away, they do it themselves.' She chewed.

Jerra kicked the bin. It toppled over, spilling its slop. The birds came.

Graffiti. Etched into the red paint. A few people watched from the pinball joint. Jerra opened the door. The clockface of the dial, the chipped receiver, dangling like a tendon. DIAL THE WORLD DIRECT with cigarette-burn punctuation. There were different graffiti on the glass and the ceiling. A chip of sky showed.

Jerra walked past the shopfronts, aching. On a picket fence, somebody had sprayed:

LIFE IS A SHIT SANDWICH
the more bread you get
THE EASIER IT IS TO TAKE

And he wondered if the bloke had seen it. Maybe he'd written it. Sean would've had something smart to say, poor bugger that he was.

Silence nicked and sliced by the sound of cutlery. Dessert on the table before anyone spoke. Jelly shivered as elbows shifted.

'Over at the Home today,' said his father, smacking the flat red of jelly with the back of his spoon.

'Hmm?'

'I said, I was over at the Home today.'

'Yeah?'

His mother glared, flushing.

'Granpa doesn't look too good.'

'And I should go over and say the last good-byes, eh?'

'Wouldn't hurt you.'

'Come on, Dad. How many times now? He pretends he's scaling the last wall every time he wants to be the centre of interest. Ol' wombat.'

His mother clapped the plates together, scraped the fat from cold chops, and threw scraps onto a sheet of newspaper.

'No way to speak about your grandfather.'

'Arr –'

'No one goes over to see him much any more,' said his father, pressing an imprint into the jelly.

'He drove them away.'

Newsprint was crumpled into a flat parcel. Dark stains appeared. It went into the kitchen tidy.

'Oh, Jerra,' said his mother, 'you just don't make sense any more. Your grandfather, now. Never complained when *you* were the favourite grandson. All the stories. About the war. Helped you write your poems.'

'Yeah, Mum.'

'Hardly spoken to him for years.'

'Since Gran died.'

'What's that got to do with it?'

A chair shuddered. His father left the table.

'I'll be going over tomorrow with your mother,' he said as he went upstairs.

'Now look what you've done.'

'I didn't do anything.'

'Story of your life, my boy,' she muttered, squeezing detergent.

'And others',' he said.

'Who do you love?'

'Nobody.'

Granma sipped.

'Course you do.'

'Boys don't.'

'Granpa did.'

'That was the olden days.'

'You love me, your ol' Granma?'

'Yes.'

'See? You're fibbing.'

Jerra squirmed at having it drawn out of him.

'What about Mum?'

'When she's not sad.'

'Dad?'

'When we go fishing. He's grumpy sometimes.'

'Who else?'

'No one.'

'Sure?'

'Auntie Jewel.'

'Oh?'

'Her pomes.'

'What about Grandad's?'

'Just blokes, blokes, blokes. They talk stupid an' never do anythink. *Got the pip wiv yearnin'* – '

Granma placed her cup roundly on the saucer. Dragonflies hovered over the hydrangeas.

His father's head beat slow time on the steering wheel. Sunlight lulled Jerra almost back to sleep.

They caught their reflections in the glass doors, and inside smelled of things Jerra remembered: postponement, the brittle smell of rotten wood, the smell of blackened lemons. Doors were open and thin heads protruded from stiff sheets, noses and cheeks twitching.

46-B. The B was coming off. Sunk in the bed, the hairless old man watched them come. His eyelashes were gone and the eyes were those of a reptile or a bird. His father's would be the same. Hands, the colour of ash, clawed the sheets.

Jerra followed in and leant on the bedside cabinet. It creaked.

'Hullo, Dad,' said his father. 'How's things?'

The mouth contracted.

'Hullo, Grandad,' said Jerra, trying to keep the lips from his own teeth.

It was cold in the little room. On the cabinet stood a cactus in a Vegemite jar. He squeezed, carefully, the firm flesh. He glanced at his mother, who smiled, lips dry and pale. A stocking was slipping, he could see. She smiled again.

'How's *he* been?' the old man rattled.

'Jerra?' his father asked. 'Oh, he's fine, aren't you, Jez?'

'Yeah.'

'Job . . .'

'What was that, Dad?' asked his mother.

'A job. Has he – ?'

'He's workin' on it,' said his father, looking sideways.

'Get him something to do, Tom.'

Thin membranes fluttered.

'I can't do it for 'im, Dad. Boy's gotta find something for himself. He's had work. Fishing. I told you about that. Might even go back one day, eh son?'

'Don't let 'im sit around. Doesn't do us any good.' The old man tightened his grip on the sheets. 'You gotta do something, Jerra.'

Jerra nodded, managing not to look away.

'Jump in.'

His mother clasped the knuckles on the sheet.

'He's doing his best, Dad,' she whispered.

'Jobs are hard to get,' said his father. 'I don't want him settlin' for anything. Like me.'

She glanced.

'I never did much,' said the old man. 'You get old 'fore you get around to doing anything.'

Jerra almost smiled, leaning on the cabinet, but the cactus caught him.

'Didn't do anything *wrong*. Not a bad man . . . sometimes you almost think you can see . . . the light on the surface . . . too far away . . . Oh, why do they give me the pills?'

Tears. A nurse came.

'Come on, Mr Nilsam. Cheer up, shall we?' She folded him neatly into the pillows. 'I think it's time for your medication. And a rest, eh? A nice rest?'

She was still at it as they went up the corridor.

the cut

The funeral, a few weeks later, was the third Jerra had been to; it was almost as hurried as Jewel's, though there was no embarrassment, only resignation and dull skies. His father was tired. Jerra noticed his patient handling of the relatives, the jolly handshakes, the meaningful sorrow-filled glances. At the cemetery Jerra's mind strayed from the burnished RSL badges and Glo-mesh handbags to Jewel's funeral where he had stepped in time with the other men, the coffin not quite resting on his shoulder, his arms aching to keep his corner up, and he saw in front of him the reddening neck of his father, red, he thought then, because his father was older than the others and was feeling the strain, but it was the same unmentioned colour that had come into his face the first day in the big house in Nedlands, and the day, a week later, that Sean moved in. Jerra often saw his father with that complexion in his younger days, standing at the window overlooking the jacarandas, hands fisted in his pockets. No, he thought, watching the serpentine movement of the Glo-mesh skin in front of him, Dad wasn't angry then, but something stuck in his guts. He knows a few things, my poor old man.

The will was read two days later.

After the relatives had left, and the lamingtons gone, Jerra's mother came up to his room with an old wooden box. Her face was dark, cut deep under the eyes. She was out of breath from the climb. Freckles of dust had settled on her forearm; her hair was limp and dull.

'There are these,' she said. 'You were to get them all, but most of them are lost.'

'What are they?' Jerra got up.

She set the gritty box down on the bed, took out the tiny, dark key and laid it on top.

'His diaries. Your father might like to look at them, later, too.'

'Finally got it sorted out, eh?'

'Hmm. Vultures, they are. Never see them otherwise still, there wasn't much to argue over. That upset them.'

'Anybody have anything to bitch about?'

'No more than usual. Mabel had a migraine, Jean was disappointed.'

'No more than usual.'

'Uncle Jim was there. Brought a gigantic wreath for the family.'

'The Power, eh? Where'd he fly in from?'

'Don't know. Nice of him, anyhow.'

'Oh, a nice man, is ol' Jimbo. He's not even family; what was he doing involved with that?'

'Bit hard, aren't you? He's done us well. He was probably just there to see we all got a fair deal. His solicitors are the executors.'

'He's a snake.' Like his wriggling son, Sean. No, he thought. He's a fox – with rabies. They both are.

She blew the tiny balls of dust from the hairs on her arm.

'Better get on with me work.' She opened the door. 'And be nice to your Dad, Jem. It's all been a bit hard on him.'

He opened the box. Inside, smelling of age and storage, were three parcels in dark, frayed envelopes. He opened them all, carefully fingering the paper. Two were bound ledger books, like thick, hard, exercise books, and the third was a small note-pad, gritty and soiled.

He glanced at the florid figures, the brownish ink. One of the larger books, ending in 1949, had been torn in half. He was revolted by the smell of the paper. He put them back in their envelopes, and the envelopes in the box.

Jerra met his father on the way down to the toilet. They nodded, his father haggard from the shift.

'Comin' down to the shack? My holidays start next week.'

'Orright. Yeah, that'd be good.'

'Have to take your chariot. Your mother's going to Mabel's.'

'Sure. Needs the run.'

'Don't leave the packing to the last minute.'

'I'll start now.'

Rain roared like a breaking wave, hammering on the tin. Jerra crossed the lino, his feet bare. He packed the bait into the freezer. A strange smell, whitebait and newsprint. He pulled the greatcoat tighter around.

His father came in, shivering.

'Have to bail the bloody boat out before we put it in the water.'

'Heavy, orright.'

A backwash of thunder. Rain spraying.

The tilly flickered on the table. Rain was still pummelling the darkness. Jerra watched his father twist and knot, holding swivels in his teeth, looping, splicing.

'Why back and over?'

'When the fish hits here, see, it flips the hook this way. Always a chance of weakening.'

Jerra held out the garlands of hooks, gangs of barbs glinting in the lamplight.

'Vicious looking – '

'Vicious eaters.' He showed the marks on his fingers. 'Tailor. Slice up the fish bigger than 'emselves.'

'Funny how the vicious ones have better meat.'

'Eat better.'

Smooth skin of the river parted behind, an incision folding back to the banks. The engine chuckled just how he remembered it from his boyhood. The river coiled out to the estuary channel. The estuary was a broad tear-drop, meeting the ocean at its narrowest point.

Jerra sat in the bow, trailing a hand over the smooth flesh of water. Old pickets stood out on either side of the channel. Across the estuary, at the deep cut to the ocean, Jerra stood and rattled the chain over. Rope burred on the gunwhale, vanishing in the green. It found bottom, slackened, and floated taut in the tide.

'Here,' his father said, 'I'll lash it.'

'I –'

'Here.' The old hands, shiny with their hardness, twisted the rope into a good knot.

From the estuary channel another motor.

'That bloke with the pelican still lives here, eh,' said Jerra, glancing up.

The hooked neck of the pelican showed plain against the grey smudge of boat and water.

Tailor scudded near the surface. His father brought one over the side. It whipped in the bottom of the boat. A moment later he had another.

'Wassamatter? Forget to bait up?'

'Do you yet.' Jerra grinned.

'Wup!'

The surface broke and his father was dragging. A whiting rippled out of the water, gills fluttering.

The bird croaked. It shoved up from the clinker-built dory, pushing it askew as it lifted, circled high, then came low over the water, following its own shadow. Between the shoulders of the breakwater, it skimmed out towards the sea. The fisherman passed them in the cut, rolling in the swell as he went into open water. His hat was over his eyes, and he stood straight in the stern, clasping the tiller.

Whitebait skipped together. It was like a handful of gravelstones hitting the water. Jerra nudged the whiting with a toe. The pale yellow pectorals fluttered.

'Nice looking fish.'

'Yeah,' said his father, bent over the gunwhale, rubbing the skin under his throat.

'Wish Mum would come, sometimes.'

73 𝒟

'She's got other things.'

'Not any more. I'm not a baby any more, and Sean's pissed off to his pooncy townhouse in South Perth.'

'Yeah.' His father bent over, a hook-shape, looking into the water.

The lead sky could support itself no longer. Rain broke the water like a million whitebait. Jerra and his father pulled their greatcoats tight, lifting collars.

'Should try for a kinghie on the tide,' his father said.

'No need.'

'Good on the clean tide.'

'Oh, these littluns'll do.' Jerra looked into the grey-green. The thought of a kinghie excited him. But frightened as well. What if he proved himself deluded?

As they were paring out the guts, dropping it over the side, scaling and washing the herring and tailor and whiting in the stinging cold water, the fisherman came back through the cut, lolling in the swell, with the pelican perched in the bow on the nets, fish grummeling down its throat. His father nodded. The fisherman may have nodded back; it was hard to tell with his hat so big and low.

'Saves on an echo-sounder,' said Jerra.

Fillets lay flat on the table. His father was trimming pieces, nipping off tails. Rain fell still. A tiny crab clattered across the lino.

'Moving around in the rain,' said Jerra.

'Little buggers.'

'Still no wind.'

'Good tomorrow.'

'If we catch the tide.'

'What about some fish?'

Jerra steered out to the estuary channel and his father took over.

'Lots of shallow banks,' he said. 'Can't be too careful.'

The channel was too murky to tell. Jerra moved up to the bow, a little peeved. Birds milled on the flats, strutting the thin strips of beach, lifting their wings.

'What about trying towards the flats?'

'The cut will be better.'

'Might be crabs at the flats.'

They headed for the cut.

In the first hour, Jerra took two big tailor on the flick-rod. Then nothing. Water surged thickly in the cut; the granite boulders of the breakwater were dull in the brief moments of sun.

'Jim owns the house in Perth, doesn't he, Dad?' It seemed a logical enough conclusion: the sudden move from the North Beach house in Jerra's last year of primary school. Mail for Jim. Jim at the funeral. All the uncomfortable talk. Sean's mocking glances.

'A favour. We did him one when Sean needed a home.'

Jerra couldn't say anything more.

Another motor. It was raining. They couldn't see.

His father slept on the bunk. As he slept, Jerra brought out the box. He laid the diaries on the table.

August 3rd, '36

Warmer today. Job shaping up well. Ellen helping organise
the deliveries. She has a good head for figures. Apples are
up. Mr Chambers says they'll fluctuate. He's probably
right. Young Jeannie is well. Five in October. Alf and
Horrie got seven dozen tailor in the river last night.
Brought some over.

   6 Eggs.

The handwriting improved and deteriorated with each entry. Days were often missed. It resumed, usually in poor writing, and got better with successive entries.

May 6th, '37

Ellen no better. Big confusion over the money. I don't
know where it goes to. They'll have me out by the end of
the week. Mabel is staying home from school to look after

Ellen. She worries that Ellen will not get well. The Rugby is playing up.

4 Eggs.

May 12th, '37

Have been helping old Henderson with the hens since the weekend. It will do for a quid until I find something else. Nothing interests me, but there is the kids. The trams just get worse. Haven't seen them so erratic since the bad times. Almost went for a job selling clocks in a shop, yesterday. The sound would send me barmy. Reminds me of the noise prawns make in the trough on the way home. Took Ellen down to the river with the kids last night. Thought it might take her mind off the worry. Will have to sell the old Rugby, though I will regret it.

2 Eggs.

Great gaps of months appeared in the rest of the entries, the last being in December 1939.

December 5th, '39

Joined AIF today. Have asked for Catering Corps, though I do not know whether or not I will get it. Sounds like a good wicket. Could not find boots to fit properly and had to settle for a size too big. Went to church yesterday. Will go again at Christmas if we don't travel.

8 Eggs.

The rest of that diary was empty yellow pages. Jerra tossed it aside and picked up the notebook. Pages were stained and gritty with dust. Many pages were folded back and torn. There was a brown stain on the cover. It could have been ink or bootpolish. Most of the erratic entries, starting from 1940, contained troop movements, rumours, and descriptions of mates. Jerra flicked through '41.

December 1st, '42
Greece has given me a bad stomach. Cooking the mush
that we do makes it worse. Am writing this because Ernie
Morris had a spare pad, and there is nothing else to do.
Ernie says it's hard cooking when you don't know salt
from dust. I don't know if I care much. There doesn't seem
to be much hope for us.

A few old photos of men drinking in a café, pinned to the page,
blurry shots of buildings and women.

April 15th, '42
Writing this from hospital (that's what they call the damn
place). Was hit in the foot by shrapnel during the bom-
bardment a few days ago. They say I might be shipped out.
What luck! Still, it hurts a lot. I will see young Tommy for
the first time. Ellen will be glad.

The last volume, though incomplete, was better preserved,
neater. The little crab scuttled under the table.

October 5th, '46
The foot has been acting up, lately. Ellen up all last night,
trying to help. Work at the markets is no good. Never
thought I would see the day when I would hate the smell
of fish.
    Saw some kids near the Causeway, paddling in the
water (yesterday). It reminded me, for some reason, of a
kid I saw in Athens, before I copped my lot. I was sitting
with a couple of mates at a café, drinking the vino. A little
boy sat on the edge of a fountain. His legs were too short
to reach the water, and I could see that he badly wanted to
get them wet. He looked at a loss, for a while, then, quite
suddenly, he jumped in feet first. I went over to see if he
was alright, and there he was, neck deep in the pool. I
offered to fish him out, but he smiled and shook his head.

Strange, those foreign kids. I would have given anything to get my boots off, big clods that they were, and get my feet wet, too.

Funny, seeing the little Wog jumping in. I'd bet a fiver he took a gamble on how deep it was. Maybe it was deeper than he expected, it was a bit . . .

The spine of the book had worn, or, as it looked, had been torn in half, and with it went the rest of the sentence. Jerra slipped it back into its envelope and closed the box. Nothing of any interest there. A drink of water was what he needed. It was the dust.

For tea they ate some tailor and whiting fillets, fried in butter. Rain fell on the roof. His father looked across in the light of the tilly-lamp.

'I've got another one,' he said.

'Another what?'

'Diary.'

'Oh?'

'One of the later ones. When he used to live here, after Gran. Best bit is – never forget it – "So-and-so date: Tom married May. Met her family. Queer mob. 4 Eggs."'

'So this shack's all you've got?'

'And what's in the Nedlands house. We own a lot of the furniture and things.'

'Not much, is it?'

'Oh, I can do this up. For when we retire. No, it's not much.'

He brought a small cloth-bound book from a cupboard.

'He threw the others out,' he said, putting it on the table. 'Do the dishes, will yer? I'm knackered. Think I'll pat the mat.'

The writing was neat and compressed. Almost every day had an entry. Jerra read one of the last.

August 5th, 1968
Young Jeremy good. Tom and May left last night. Fished for bream down near the Brewery. Caught two apiece.

Taught him a bit of C. J. Dennis. He can remember the
first verse. Will write his own if he gets past the first
verse. He's got a soul that boy. And he thinks no one knows.

Jerra sat back in the chair. His chest. He must have swallowed
a bone. He closed the book.
'Spring song,' he muttered. '"A Spring Song"':

> The world 'as got me snouted jist a treat;
>   Crool Forchin's dirty left 'as smote me soul;
> An' all them joys o' life I 'eld so sweet
>   Is up the pole.
> Fer, as the poit sez, me 'eart 'as got
> The pip wiv yearnin' fer – I dunno wot.

Why doesn't anyone tell me anything, he asked himself. Why
do they just let you go on and then give you a letter or something
or write it down in a poem instead of telling you?
He went to bed, comfortable in the pretence that he didn't know.

'We're late for the sea tide,' said his father in the bow.
'Didn't hurt to sleep in.'
The boat cut the brownish river. The pickets in the channel were
rotting stumps of teeth. In the cut, the water was still, the anchor
rope slack as the boat turned on itself. Sun burnt through the film
of cloud, lighting up the water. It hurt their eyes. Plip! Whitebait
being chased, they both knew. Jerra clicked his tongue. His father
nodded, not lifting his lids.
The bird croaked. The long boat slid over the shallow banks,
the Hat punting with an oar, watching the bird's shadow on the
water. It wafted around in a loose curve, without moving a feather,
beak flat against the sky.
Jerra saw swirling spectrums of whale oil in the water, purple
and yellow, even when the sun was sucked back into the clouds.
He heard the slop of the net on the water.
The line tightened, singing, Jerra had a fish, struggling off at

79 *⏧*

an angle, going deep. He swung it up out of the water and into the boat. It beat itself against the boards. Then another, and another. His father shifted. The Hat was poling the boat away from the net. Corks jostled on the surface.

'Must've seen something in those shallows,' said his father.

'Him or the bird?'

Jerra smiled. His father glanced across. Inside the perimeter of shimmying corks, the water was coming to the boil. A tail slapped the water. The Hat beat the water with an oar.

The bird-shadow flickered across. Jerra pulled in another tailor, the oar beating and slapping as he baited up. The pelican croaked playfully. He hoped it wouldn't scare the fish off. He saw it settle just outside the perimeter of the net. Fish boiled the water. The pelican was becoming excited.

It rained, heavy.

'Not going too good?' he smiled.

He looked up. It was hard to see. He saw feathers and the oar coming down on the water driving the fish into the net. Feathers ruffling, excited. Something tearing? Jerra couldn't make out the sound. Beak skyward; pink webs of feet. The bird was inside the net, churning about in the living mass. Churning. Then, the oar not hitting water. Blemishes appeared on the water outside the net from a volume of escaping fish. It was caught up in the net; a bumper catch fleeing. Shouts. Rain fell harder. Frightened croaks. Where? The rain was blinding. The bag-throat appeared again, quivering. For a moment he saw nothing again and looked away. He looked again to see the bird-rag on the surface and flagellant rain and the spreading feathers.

All around their boat, fish were jumping, flattening themselves on the water. Jerra pulled in another as the anchor chain cleared the water.

Out of the brown river the tide was oozing into the estuary towards the sea. Brown pickets. Jerra sat in the bow, wishing they had a bigger motor.

hooks

Town was gritty with the dry powder of leaves rasping along the footpaths. Windows offered, reflected, but he was reluctant to look. Horns and tinny music. From the railway bridge he watched the trains slither and jolt, their roofs dusty below. Often he wondered how far down they were. Since a child, he had wanted to drop something, a peppermint or a stone, onto the carriages as they passed. He wondered whether anyone had jumped. They had from other places. And made the papers.

Across the railway, he wandered through the sleazier streets, past dead neon, the tight restaurants, clubs, bars. A man opened the door of a wine bar, pinning it back with his broom. Bearded and weary, he nodded as Jerra passed, but got no response.

He completed the circle; crossed at the western bridge.

'Granpa's teachin' me C. J. Dennis.'

'Oh? Is he?'

'Yep.'

'Gone off love poems?'

'Oh, no,' he said, pulling at a sock. 'Love's orright.'

'Orright, eh?'

'That's how people get married.'

She smiled, long legs shining in the sun.

'Yes.'

'I'd marry you, Auntie Jewel. You're orright.'

'Don't worry, Jem, I'd take you up. You're the only man for me.

You and your old man are okay. Your Mum's got a good deal.'
  'Yeah, she's orright, too.'

He went home.
  In his room, he sat with his head against the marked wall. What a bunch of cripples, he thought. To resort to writing diaries and letters . . . and bloody books; he looked up at hopeless, drunken Malcolm Lowry whose spine still protruded from the tightly packed shelf.
  He sniffed his hands. They smelt of buses and handrails and dust, not fish; they didn't even smell of *him*.
  He sighed and got on his knees beside the bed and pulled the bottom drawer from the desk. Feeling in the space behind it, he worried out a long manila envelope. He put it on his bed and was about to open it when he remembered the door and got up and locked it.
  He shuffled through the letters, reading excerpts.

Dearest Jerra,
  Thank you for your lovely visit. It must be quite a shock to you. You didn't show it, of course. You never have. It's nice to think of yourself as a tough little biscuit. Your poems are better. Quite sexy, some of them. I didn't know you were so advanced. I'm sorry about saying what I did. I'm not used to the smell of fish, that's all. I expect you'll be all hurt now and wear a screechingly clean collared-shirt, have red-raw hands and shoes and all, next time you come. You'd better not! I'd feel awful. And I wouldn't recognise you, anyway!
  Send me some more poems when school becomes a torture.
      Much love,
      Jewel

A letter from Rome. There was a trip after the first 'breakdown'.

. . . will be home in May to see you all and show you what
an immaculate conception is all about. Do you know
whether businessmen are supposed to have more prostate
trouble than other middle-aged men? Look it up in your
Biol. for me, will you? There must be some excuse for it.
  People here are entertaining in this city. Really, my boy . . .

Then, something from hospital marked August '76. Not the mental
hospital; a private hospital by the river.

. . . Your poems, my lovely man, are well-meant, but
lacking in truth. *I know* what it means to have my insides
torn, and it's not like those words. Replace 'collapse' with
'mutilate' . . .

. . . *Means*? why the preoccupation? Irrelevant. Sounding
like your father when young. Means are painful delays, ask
my doctors. Ask the saints. Don't fuss so . . . Let's not
have ideals, let's surrender to the men of *Ends*. Hence the
joke at business luncheons about getting your end up. *They*
are ends in themselves. END HEADS. Eh? . . .

After the quick move to Heathcote:

. . . Repetition is a good device. Good God, it's a real
enough pattern! He would have been a crazy beautiful
baby Latin. Sean, my loving son, would be mostly
unmoved. He has decided that he is of illegitimate origin
which explains your confusion. He has been convinced, of
course. A beautiful foreign bastard brother shouldn't
bother him, then. Curious the minds of boys that are men
and men that are boys. Why are they never people, though?

Jerra read a few sentences from the months that haunted him.
Was he mad then? Madder than her? He sighed and read.

It's beautiful when it happens. O, of course. Of.
Course. Do not be afraid, my Jeramiah. I think you
always wanted . . . yes. This is indestructible! *We* are!

At the bottom of the page were two stanzas plagiarised from
Sylvia Plath's "Lady Lazarus" (he only discovered its true origin
in a tutorial at Uni). It froze him still.

> *The second time I meant*
> *To last it out and not come back at all*
> *I rocked shut*
> *As a seashell.*
> *They had to call and call.*
> *And pick the worms off me like sticky pearls.*

And there was one thin envelope, puce, with cambric pig-
mented texture, that he would not open. It was postmarked
February 1977, when Jerra was away on the boats, trying to forget
and grow up and *do* and please and forget. It was something he
neither needed now, nor wanted to refresh his memory with. He
promised to let go. His problems and everyone else's. Maybe Sean
was right.

'You gotta live,' he told himself lamely.

Jerra went out – back into town – wandering.

Smoke twisted on itself, rising and falling in the dimness. In one
corner, near the open, gutless Wurlitzer, a table was free. Jerra
bought a burgundy and sat, glancing at the initials carved into
the piano. A guitarist was hunching into a long, slow blues, his
head above the clouds of smoke.

> *Lord it's a mean ol' world*
> *When you livin' o' ba yoursel';*
> *If ya caint get the one that you lovin',*
> *Then you gotta put up wi' somebuddy*
> *else.*

The wine was warm; he'd never drunk it before and it hardly wet his throat as it went down, each bitter swallow. The blues moaned to a tortured finish, and Jerra clapped, alone, self-consciously. The guitarist nodded, and mumbled about Walter Jacobs as he tuned, squinting at the ivory tuning keys.

A chair burped on the boards.

'Anyone sitting here?' She had long hair, a glass of port and a leather shoulder bag.

'No,' he mumbled. 'Siddown.'

Hair and bag swung down into the seat across the table; the sort of chair they pop out a hundred at a time, with that rugged, individual look. The slide whined on the strings. Elmore James.

Wennawekupinnermornin abelieveadus'mablooz!

Next to him, the freckled hand beat time on the pine table. Port jiggled, a rosy quiver in the shapely little glass. There was a fingerprint near the rim, quite clear. The guitarist stuttered, calling his baby back home. She smiled lightly, rolling a cigarette, and Jerra drained the bitterness from his glass as the guy believed his time weren't long and sent 'is babe a tel'gram.

And they both clapped at the finish, Jerra feeling less foolish. It was a good old song.

'This is a smooth little joint,' she said while the guitarist was tuning again.

He smiled, looking around at the beards and batik.

There were lines under her eyes, and dusty freckles on her forehead and cheeks that made it difficult to guess her age. She might have been older or younger than him. Older, he thought, noting the weariness and the way she held the glass with her thumb poking over the edge, like shearers he had seen in those cruddy little pubs out east.

Another blues. It swayed on itself, building and falling, chunka-chunka-whine-wizz, glass slicking up and down the fretboard.

'Muddy Waters,' she said into his ear, as if he didn't know. Still, he thought, it was nice. He smiled and nodded, lured under by

85

the swirling rhythm. The wine was swilling around inside him as he stomped his foot. Again, they clapped, together and alone. There was a break. Jerra bought a port, holding the little eye-dropper glass awkwardly, and sat back, not minding the smoke so much. She smiled and sipped.

> . . . Do you understand these letters? You show no sign of understanding me, sometimes . . .

'Well,' she asked, pulling back a swirl of hair with short little fingers. 'What do you think of him?'

Jerra licked the edge of the glass. The port was warm and sweet; it reminded him of neat Ribena.

'He's not bad, actually. Plays better than he sings.'

'You want a smoke?' She had small hands.

'Don't smoke, thanks.'

'Good idea,' she said, as they all said, blowing a stream from the side of her mouth.

She talked about smoking and health in general; she was a vegetarian, concerned about the toxins in meat and the garbage people devour following the mindless instructions of television advertising. Jerra agreed, listening uncritically, curious about jasmine tea, Rajneesh and Poona, but paying more attention to the fine powder of freckles on her skin.

'Do vegies eat fish?' he asked.

'They do now.'

'You mean they didn't once?'

'But it's okay now.'

'It's in this year, then, is it?' he said, making an attempt at dry sophistication.

> . . . I didn't know you were quite so advanced . . .

She hit him on the shoulder with the back of her hand. It wasn't an unpleasant sensation.

'What's so special about fish?' she asked, looking about.

'Dunno,' he admitted. 'I just can't imagine anyone not eating fish.'

'Some people don't like it, you know,' she said patronisingly.

'That's 'cause they can't be stuffed picking out the bones.' He laughed, self-conscious; it seemed a bit of a hopeless comment. 'No, I s'pose they don't like it, some people.'

'Really coming up with some gems, aren't we?' She cuffed him across the shoulder again, brushing against his old corduroy jacket. He felt like grabbing her hand and feeling the little fingers, freck-led prawns, wriggling in his palm.

'You ever done any?' he asked suddenly.

'What?'

'Fishing.'

'Yes. As a girl. A few years ago, yes.' She laughed. 'Of course I couldn't guess that you do a bit yourself.'

'Yeah,' he said enthusiastically. 'Ever since I could sit up and hold a line.'

There was a pause during which Judy appeared restless. Jerra fidgeted.

'Did you like it?' he asked at length. 'When you went, I mean. Fishing.'

'Yes. Yeah. Sure.' She looked at him, mildly curious.

'Why?'

'Pardon?'

'Why did you like it? What was the best thing?'

'The best thing?' She plucked at her skirt which flowed in dark ripples to her ankles. She squinted, mouthing, and Jerra watched, almost annoyed by the way she took her time. 'Well, I always fished from a boat – a big one – with my father and brothers. Canal Rocks, Hamelin Bay, places like that, catching skippy and herring with handlines. All those tangles.'

'Skippy, yeah.' He would have like to hold one shivering in his hand, now. Not in a boat.

'I think the best thing was when you pull them over the side into the bottom of the boat, and then take the hook out.'

'The hook?'

'I was taught to hold the fish against my leg. Like this, see? My old man was pretty good at it. When he was younger. Like this,' she said, pinning the small leather bag to the side of her thigh. 'Hold the fish with your right hand, and unthread the hook with your left.'

'Well?' He didn't know whether she was telling him how to do it, or if she was merely reciting something.

She held the bag flat against the gathered skirt.

'Power. The moment you take the hook out and hold that fish in your hand, you have a lot of power.'

Jerra smiled.

'At that moment, you decide the future of that fish, whether to put it in the bag, or throw it back. Life or death. Like . . . political masturbation.'

Jerra laughed, blowing all the air out, holding his legs, like when he'd taken an elbow in the guts playing back-pocket for the school. Then he was sorry. Sean used to say it, anyway. Some of their port had spilled with his rocking.

'Well, what's wrong with that?'

'Nothing. Really.'

'Well?' She could have been hurt. Or pretending, that little freck-led forehead crinkling.

'Something wrong with that theory.'

She plopped the bag on the table, careful of the stain.

'The power bit, or the idea of masturbation?'

'The power bit, I think.' He had to smile. He watched her finish her port, tipping it in little sips with her fingers around the edge of the glass and her thumb up.

'Sorry about laughing.'

'Okay. Not all that serious.'

'It was a bit off.'

She set the glass down carefully on the table.

'Well, you did ask me.'

'I did that, orright.'

'Anyway, I have to go,' she said, easing the bag onto her shoulder.

'Coming here tomorrow?'

'Don't know,' she murmured, sliding her glass around the table.

'We could talk some more. About fishing. And I could think some more about your theory.'

'Oh yeah.'

The freckles disappeared when she stood up. They were so small.

. . . Do not be afraid my Jeramiah

Jerra's hands were numb on the wheel as he pulled into the rutty dirt patch. He switched off, looking at the STAFF ONLY sign with the footprint in the middle. There were tears of dew on the frosty blisters of paint. The engine was cooling with that clicking that people made when they slept on their backs. He slammed the sucked-in door of the VW extra hard; it was getting a bit tough to close. A car started somewhere, a grinding whirr of starter motor, a brief fart, and silence. It started the second time, wheezing, the choke out six feet. Sixty feet, he thought.

He pulled his coat off as he went in through the back door that connected with Al's house. The dunny was between the shop and the back door, probably a security measure; he wondered if they had the septic on, or if they ever emptied it, though he never dared find out. A generation of thick turds packed into one confined space, behind that peeling door. Even the paintwork felt it. It was a relief to escape into the stench of sweets and cold meat pies.

Al met him at the Coke fridge, rubbing his hands on the apron that was stiff with filth. His hands were blue.

'Two mornings, an' not late, eh? I don' belief it.'

'Said I would be on time, didn't I?'

Al didn't look much like an Italian. It was the moustache, Jerra decided; he didn't have the moustache. And he was probably taller than five one. He could have been forty, he might have been fifty.

'Pies in the oven,' Al said at his blue hands.

Jerra separated the frozen pies and piled them onto the tray. Could have dropped one and broken a toe.

Then there were the sausage rolls, the pasties, and then the frozen red frankfurters he dropped like pink fingers into the big scummy pot. Rosa came in as he was piling up the mountains of potato chips in their loud orange packets.

' 'Ello, Jerra,' she said, finding something in her teeth as she crossed to the till. 'Big test today.' She laughed. 'Sat'dee makes yer or breaks yer.'

'Can't wait.'

Al was watching, cleaning his hairy ear with the rubber end of a pencil.

Rosa was fat, a distended, turgid hot-dog about to burst its red skin. Her hands often strayed over the open boxes, smelling of the hard sweetness of lollies. Jerra pretended not to notice.

At nine Al went out the back to read the paper on his stinking dunny. Jerra heard the noises that disgusted him.

Rosa began at him again. She thumped him on the shoulder, and he could feel her mouth stinging his cheek.

'Two years of Uni,' she said laughing, 'for this?'

'Yep.'

'Dad took me outta school when I was thirteen.'

'Why?'

'Said it would be better leaving to work for him, than go on with school and end up on the dole.'

'Hmph.'

'Maybe he was right, I dunno,' she said, sucking something red, round and sweet. Her dress seemed to belong to someone else. Like the bags they put the fruit in, fruit always soft and a bit bruised.

'Reckon I shoulda gone on, you know.'

'Yeah?' The pies were softening. He wondered if they really were roo meat. They stank like it.

'So many oppertunities.'

He felt the pastry warming, the juice melting out of the meat. They probably picked them up off the side of the road, he thought, smiling.

'No opportunities, really.'

'Oh, carm on,' she said, scratching. 'You don't appreciate what you could of had.'

'Arr.' If the customers only knew why they tasted of duco.

'No. You could of done somethink.'

'What?'

'I dunno. There must of been somethink. Yer mad if yer can't find somethink to do wuth yourself.'

'I have. I work here.' He unbolted the door. The bell clunked.

'Arr, yer mad. You must be stupid, or yer haven't looked.'

'How the hell would you know?' He slammed the liquorice allsorts onto the Laminex. 'Shit, Rosa, what would you know?'

Rosa fiddled pasties onto a tray, thick steam rising into her face. She lifted the damp hair out of her eyes. Her face was pink.

'You're weak as piss, Jerra.'

The bell clonged, a turd hitting the water. He braced behind the counter.

The deli was on a street corner. There were houses neatly spaced along the street, and in the next street there was a school. A street or two down, there was a factory that made doors. As lunch time neared, the mountains of potato chips crumbled, the milkshaker screamed without stopping for a breath, and aniseed balls scattered and clattered as more black-toothed children, smiling through their gaps, came and went on the lino that gripped their thongs, tacky with Coke.

Al scowled at all the customers, young or old, slamming their pies down on the counter in their brown bags, rattling the lollies into little white bags with careful underestimation, baring his teeth to the children humming and hahing over two for one, three for five or how much can I get for two cents. Jerra knew it didn't matter a damn to Al who gave them all the same and said he wished he was a dentist.

They worked under the tinny snaffle of the transistor that perched high on the back shelves. Jerra poured the thickshakes, watching the stuff unwind and settle like castor oil. He sorted ham and salad, sneezed wrapping curried egg, and slapped the beef and pickle together. He felt the coins, hot from the customers' hands, and cursed the twenty dollar notes passed over, with Kingsford Smith smirking, for a Mars Bar or chips. All day. All day. All day. Then wiping the Coke from the floor, and scraping the coagulated sauce from the counter.

He gave the old Veedub a kick, feeling the notes in his pocket, and spun her out of the dirt patch, hopping it off the kerb with a chirp.

'Why doesn't anyone tell him the truth?'

'It's between Sean and his Dad,' said his mother, pegs between her teeth.

'Someone's gotta tell him!'

'He wouldn't listen, Jerra.'

'No, he wouldn't,' he admitted.

'He thinks his father's right. That's all he's got left.'

'And it's worse than nothing.'

She bit on the pegs, shaking her head.

'And he doesn't want to find out, Mum. Why doesn't anyone want to find anything?'

'They get old,' she said spreading a heavy, gently steaming sheet on the line, holding it with an elbow and pegging one end. 'And Sean's got old too soon.'

'No. It's giving up. No one gets old too soon.'

'I figured it out,' he said, putting two ciders on the table.

'What?' She seemed distracted.

She was wearing jeans and a quilted coat; the same stuff they made the old sleeping bags out of, he noted. Her boots were freckled with mud. A singer was howling about a big brass bed and the smoke poured on itself, boiling to the low ceiling. A different singer, all beard and eyes.

'Your theory.'

'Oh, that.'

'Yeah. I figured it was wrong because there was a . . . what do you call it? . . . a variable. The fish.'

'Eh?' She glanced at him over her glass.

'The fish. You said you had power over it; but it's not really true. Put him in the bag. Fine, he's dead; you scale him, gut him, eat him.

But if you throw him back there's no guarantee he's going to live.'

She was still looking at him, an eyebrow up.

'You have been a busy boy.'

'The fish might survive the hook and the exposure and take off. Or he might be weakened and be easy prey for a bigger fish, or he might die in a couple of minutes, just from shock.'

'So, the fish decides its own fate?'

'Sort of. Maybe the fish's strength, or something else; but whether he lives or dies won't be decided by throwing him back.' There was nothing to him like that grunt of surrender, the gentle collapse from deep within, and the mate rolling off into the deep at the precise second. Nothing. Like knowing or believing in subtle defeat.

She smiled.

'So, what does it all mean?'

'Dunno.'

She was looking around, her lower lip uncurling, tongue pushing from behind.

'Geez, this is a weird joint.'

'Lost in the sixties.'

'Yeah, the sixties.'

'You'd hardly remember.'

'An' you admit remembering?'

'Oh, bits. And pieces.'

'Maybe I don't remember. Bit young.' He drank his cider. It was rotten stuff, really, sweet enough to make you sneeze. They drank it at school parties, hidden in their greatcoats, cold and hard against their chests. A bottle left them flat – stung, on the back lawns of mates whose parents were away. Chundering in the long grass, against the rickety pickets.

'Don't they sell beer?'

'Awful stuff.'

'This is worse.' Dugite phlegm.

They watched each other. She was making a lot of enjoying the cider. The bubbles in the glass were like raindrops falling up instead of down.

'He's playing bloody Bob Dylan, again,' Jerra said.

'Falling back on the party favourites.' She ran the edge of her hand along the grain of the pine. 'So, by putting the fish back, feeling you've done a good thing, you could be killing it, anyway.'

'Yeah.'

'Gets a bit hard to tell right from wrong.'

'I s'pose it hits you sooner or later.'

'I don't know your name.'

'What?'

'I don't even know your name.'

'Oh, Jerra. Jerra Nilsam.'

'Jerra?'

'Jerra.'

'What sort of name is that?'

'Dunno.'

'Sounds like wood.'

'Yeah, they reckon.'

'I'm Judy Thyme.'

She got up and bought drinks, jeans tight against her calves.

The music lapped around them, smoke and noise producing a closeness that half-stifled, half-excited him. He studied her face, her tiny freckles, the crack in her thumbnail, the way she moved him through an endless series of conversations, breaking them down, word by word, tracing back tiny links that became new topics themselves. He loved being guided, and went whichever way she did.

At closing, they picked their way through the fallen bodies and tables, and onto the street, where the cold air fronted them, the gutters wet, and the take-away menus from next door plastered soggily to the footpath.

'You got a car?' he asked as he rubbed his hands together. It was colder than it had been for a long time. Parking meters gleamed.

She shook her head.

'Swanbourne. Too far?'

'No worries.' His toes were numb; he had only worn thongs. The cold air was making his nose run, and he sniffed quietly.

In the alley between the wine bar and the opp. shop there was a figure up against the wall, someone wheezing as if having just run a long stretch. He looked again and it was two bodies, one rasping the other against the damp wall, feet shifting as the gutters trickled, seeping.

. . . my Jeramiah.

The VW stood alone in a parking lot by the railway line. A train passed, slow and brightly lit, with no one inside. A procession of lighted carriages rocking through the city. Jerra wrenched the door open.

'How long have you had this?'

'A few years.'

'Given you trouble?'

'First country trip I ever took it on. Got as far as Williams and it passed out.'

'What was wrong?'

'Country air, I s'pose. Hay fever or something. Funny ol' bus.'

The upholstery was cold and the beaded windscreen misty with breath. The roads in town were glistening, lit red and orange in neon flickers, and it was hard for him to keep his mind on the blinking reds of the road and talk as well. The river was black, awash with the lights of the freeway and the brewery. Passing the Uni with its stopped-clock tower lit against the black of night, he felt a hand on his leg. It could have been on his knee, but it was difficult to pinpoint. He didn't look, and it was harder to drive. She was closer and the cab had warmed. He didn't feel much like talking. He watched the slick, glistening road, listening to the muted roar of the engine.

He pulled into the driveway she pointed out, leaving the motor running.

'Thanks for the lift,' she said without letting go his leg. 'Coffee?' Her face was green in the light of the speedometer that never worked.

'I'd better be off.'

'I can make it with whisky.'

'Some other time, eh?'

'Yeah, fine.'

He leant over and kissed her clumsily on her mouth or ear, he couldn't tell, her hair in his face.

'Ring you?' His lips were cold, and hard to get around his teeth.

'No phone. I'll ring you.'

He mumbled the number and she climbed down. He shoved it into reverse and the van shook a little as the headlights lit her. She went up to the front door, lit sharp in the shadows. She waved.

The sheets took a while to warm, and the pillow stung his ear.

A lot further down this time. Deeper than he had anticipated. Strands of weed brushed his cheek in the dark, and as he felt his way down the rock bit cold on his hand. There was nothing. He went in darker and found something soft. It trembled, the skin almost tightening. He rolled it over, the legs fanning wide, and saw the open slit reflecting green on the backs of his hands. Scars of old slashes gathered, pale on the flaccid pulp. Navel a stab-hole. In a dowdy gown, she was arching pathetically, spreading her speckled hair, clutching, and he was saying Baaaaaaas-taaaaaarrrrrds! inside; and she wanted him to say something nice because nobody did any more. But she wasn't her. Just a bald slit and light showing through. They hadn't made her different, or even someone else; just nothing. And he was smiling, hand beneath the open neck that was once curved like a beach, kissing. It giggled, then groaned like dying, but she was dead already, before the butchery, and he wished he was now. He hated himself because she wasn't properly aware, because she couldn't tell half the time, and he was no different from the others taking advantage, helping to destroy, helping her in the delusion.

NO

Each morning, Al's dunny was worse. Jerra could smell it easily from the dirt of the parking lot, as if each turd was calling out for a septic tank, dying from claustrophobia. He had never been in there. A whole day's wait was nothing to what must lie behind that fly-caked door.

'There he is,' called Al, almost friendly. 'The early boy. Ready to work hard, eh?'

'Dying for it,' he replied, watching Rosa opening a new canister of ice-cream. The shop was warm from the ovens, but never warm enough to take the blue out of your hands.

Jerra stacked the fridge with Coke, and clacked together blocks of pies. His hands wouldn't warm, even when slushing hot water over the floors. Rosa was silent. You have to feel a bit sorry for her, hiding those chockie drops in her puffy palms like that, he thought to himself.

Having his lunch break once, Al sat next to him smoking a putrid Italian cigarette, leaving Rosa with the after-lunch mob.

'Rosa tell me you been to the Uni.'

'Couple of years.'

'Why quit? Not smart enough, eh?'

It was on again.

'Didn't seem worth sticking at.'

Al sucked on his cigarette. The smoke knotted around the room.

'So you *were* smart enough. But not enough to stay. Leaving so smart?'

Jerra shifted on the boxes. KIT KAT stamped on the one under him.

'Thought it was the smartest thing to do.'

'Knockin' back the chance?'

'For what?'

'To *be* somebody.'

He felt the corrugations in the sides of the cardboard, ribs under his fingers.

'Nothing to do with it.'

'So you work 'ere, in a shop that I have to run to be somebody. Al the Ding. He runs the deli down the road. You waste time doing things like this.'

'Not a waste.'

'How would you know? You done nothink! Got brains – so you work in a lousy shop.'

Jerra bit. The gristly mince was going cold. He swallowed quickly, trying not to taste duco.

'*You* work in a lousy shop.'

Al grubbed his smoke out on the grey wall. Small rings crept around the bulb on the ceiling.

'I got no choice. There's nothink else.'

'Same. For both of us.'

Al stood and kicked the boxes, planting a hole in a red K.

'Rosa is right. You *are* stupid. You donna what choice is!'

Jerra took a breath. Al was gone. He finished the pie in the smoky little room.

Rods stuck out stiff from the granite of the mole. The sea outside the harbour was chopped by a sou'westerly. The sun was dropping quickly and, here and there, lamps began to glow. At dark there was no sound but the wind in the rocks and the slow click-click of the reels winding in. A launch passed, lit brightly. Snatches of music stuttered in the wind. Jerra saw his mother's hands in the lamplight, the thick needles moving over the brown wool; she sat in the lee of a coarse boulder, out of the chill. Insects beat themselves on the hot glass. Next to him a reel clicked, the ratchet turning over slowly.

'Anything?'

'No,' said his father, hair ruffled by the wind, wisps of grey shining in the periphery of the light.

'See the paper today?' his mother asked.

'No.' He reeled in a little.

'More bad news.'

'Bloody Russians,' said his father, swinging the gang of hooks up onto the rock. 'There'll be war soon.'

'If the Yanks have their way,' said Jerra.

'Conscription, too, the way the Liberals are.'

'That'd be awful.'

'Could do some good. Absorb some of the unemployed, or something.'

'Send 'em off to the Middle East. Vietnam absorbed a few. Like a bloody Wettex.'

'Who needs a war?' his mother said. 'There's kids killing themselves these days. In a phone booth, last week or before.'

'It wasn't because he needed a bloody war to go to.'

His mother was silent. He could hear the needles clicking between gentle gusts. His father cast out, the mulie spinning out into the darkness. A small white splosh. Jerra reeled in, checked his bait, and cast out languidly, dropping just short of his father's splash.

'Bit more flick.'

'Don't worry, Dad, I'll get it one day.' He laughed, glancing over his shoulder. His mother was looking down at her hands. 'Who's it for?'

'You.'

'Oh?'

'Been knitting it ever since you got back from South.'

'Vee-neck?'

'Course. Learnt my lesson.'

'It itches my throat.'

'Father's the same. At least he'll wear his.'

Wham! Jerra's rod whipped down, almost into the water. He jerked back and took up the slack, but there was nothing.

'Strike?'

'Gone.'

'What was it?'

'Big an' fast, whatever it was.'

'Anything's too fast for you two.'

His father reeled in, chuckling. He turned into the lamplight to bait up. Jerra reeled in as his father cast out. Bait gone. He impaled a frozen mulie on the line of barbs.

'More flick, this time.'

'Yes, Dad.' He flicked the bail-arm over and drew the rod back. It bowed and snapped forward, line whistling. A white pock showed, quite a way further out than his father's.

'Better?'

'Not bad.'

'Clowns,' murmured his mother.

'Haah!'

Line unspooling with a whine, his father braked and dragged the big rod back.

'What is it?'

'Big.'

The rod arched, straining to reach the water. His father stepped back and took slack. Jerra could hear his little gasps.

'Get the gaff!'

Jerra went back to the rocks, still holding his rod, and grabbed the long gaff.

'Doubling back!' yelled his father, reeling. The rod straightened. As the fish turned again, it went back into the crook.

Jerra watched his father trying to straighten, hair in his eyes. His knees were bent and the baggy trousers were flapping.

'And again. Gaff.' He was puffing.

'Yeah.'

'Lost him again.' Straining.

Jerra reeled in, put his rod down and stood ready with the gaff. Line hummed out again.

'Wassamatter?'

'Nothin', jus . . .'

Reel screaming.

'Hold it!'

'I –'

Jerra dropped the gaff and grappled the rod away, almost losing
it as his father let go and sagged back into his wife's arms. He
dragged sideways to break the run, and reeled. The rod was alive,
quaking. Jerra heard his mother behind. Water broke and there
was a tail-slap. Then the fish ran at the rocks and he could hardly
reel in fast enough. He gaffed it, one handed, up onto the dry rock.

'Bonito!'

The thin, whippy tail hit him in the shin.

'Give me a hand,' his mother said. 'Come on, Tom.'

'Hey, Dad, how's that?'

His father didn't look up.

'You okay?'

'Jerra –' his mother hissed.

'Bit of a turn's all.'

Jerra laughed.

'He did yer, orright, eh?'

She glared.

'Fifteen pound of 'im.'

'Nah.'

'Big *enough*.' Jerra laughed.

His father said nothing, grey faced, breathing short and shallow.

'How've you been?' Judy asked him.

'Orright.' He could never think of anything to say on the phone.

'The deli?'

'A ball. Make it a career.'

'Hmm.'

'And what've you been doing?'

'Nothing much.'

'Mm-hm.'

'Dinner?'

'Orright, sure.'

Bitten fragments of talk. He hung up, wondering. He shivered.
Winter would be a long one this year.

It was so cold in the morning that Jerra wore gloves to drive to work. But he had to take them off at the shop. Hygiene, Al said. Jerra's fingers were bluer in a few minutes than they had ever been. They ached from working the ovens and fridges at the same time.

Al came in off the dyke, sullen.

'Move your arse today, boy. Friday they spend big.'

The morning ached slowly on. Near lunch time, the kids and the mothers with prams, and the overalled men from the factory, began to straggle in, buying extra chips and cigs to last the weekend. The chips crackled, pies were slapped on the counter, bottle-tops jangled in the bin, and milkshakes were snorted up through straws by grimy children, arguing colour and length and three-for-one.

At the peak, the counter was writhing with heads and hands, calling for a thousand different things, and rattling change and lollies in bags. A big man from the factory shoved kids aside, forcing his way to the counter. A boy, short and dark, complained, glancing up at the man.

'Boofhead,' said the little face.

The man took him by the collar and flicked him under the ear. Spilling his coppers on the floor in a shower, the boy fled. Laughing, the man scooped up a few coins, held them in his hand for the other children to see, and pocketed them. The children murmured. A lady walked out, muttering 'Bloody oaf' over and over. Rosa was busy at the other end of the counter. Jerra went over to the pie oven where Al tapped impatiently on the glass door.

'You see that? What a bastard. Shall I serve him?'

'Has he got money?'

Jerra looked away. If he didn't before, he has now, he thought.

'Yeah.'

'He's a customer.'

'You can't let a prick like that get away with it. What about the bloody kids!'

Al opened the oven door.

'Serve him.'

'An' you think I'm weak as piss,' he muttered, going back.

The big man was at the counter, leaning heavily on the Laminex in his greasy overalls, twiddling the straws in their chrome canister. Jerra avoided him, serving kids on either side. The factory worker tapped hard on the Laminex with a coin, that irritating, pecking sound.

'Arr, carm on. Serve some bloody customers!'

Jerra ignored him. Coaxing the little heads to speak and lingering over their orders, he fussed unnecessarily on their behalf. He was itching for something. From the corner of his eye he saw a blue arm reaching into the Coke fridge. Jerra knew now what he was itching for. He dropped his whole weight on the heavy lid, jamming the man's arm up to the elbow. He roared. Jerra saw the corned beef in his teeth and leant heavier on the lid.

'Getchafuckenandoff!'

'What's it doin' in the fridge?' he yelled back, smiling at the children who were more terrified than impressed.

The face brightened in its reds and whites as Jerra pressed harder, then the other hand, out of reach, smacked the straw canister to the floor, spraying straws and children in all directions. Then, despite Jerra's weight, the man dragged his arm out of the fridge, taking off a flap of skin, and threw a tall jar of penny-sticks onto the floor. It shattered, glass skittering on the linoleum. Jerra was no longer smiling.

'You little barsted!'

Rosa screamed. As he backed away, Jerra knew that Al was not there; he had an idea where he would be. He groped along the side bench for a weapon. Anything. As the big man straddled the counter, Jerra fumbled up a cold bottle of Coke, feeling the teeth of the bottle-top in his palm as he slammed it down onto the overalled shin. Another scream. Not Rosa. The man purpling. Blood from the arm. Jerra pounded him frantically on the buttocks as he continued dragging himself over. Very scared now, Jerra retreated behind the chocolate shelves where he caught a glimpse of Al, scuttling and locking.

Something shattered. Rosa screaming again.

'He's got a bottle!' she wailed.

As the bloody sleeve appeared, the teeth of glass held like a knife with many blades, Jerra moved back further, wanting to be sick and ready at the same time, backing into the dimness of a corner with a thirty-cent Coke chilling his palms. Overalls. He sprang out, rammed the bottle hard and high between the man's legs, and kicked wildly in the same place and others as the legs bent like paper straws. A hand went around his throat but opened as the man fell. Grunting and gargling, the body pumped on the linoleum, twitching, sucking in air.

'Rosa,' he called, very quiet, shaking.

'Is he dead? Where's Dad?'

Jerra kicked the broken bottle-neck from the writhing man's fingers. It slithered into a corner.

'Dad orright?' Rosa came.

'He's just locking the strongbox.' That bubbling noise sickened him.

Al appeared.

'Got a smart-arse, eh?'

'Oh, shit, Al.'

'Watcher make trouble for?'

'Oh, come on!'

Al went back behind the shelves. Jerra leant against the counter, staring around the empty shop, keeping an eye on the stricken factory man. Al came back with the strongbox, unlocking it again.

'See you were lookin' after things,' Jerra sneered.

'Rosa was right. You're *real* stupid!' He flung the box open and snatched out a few twenties and some smaller notes. 'Here.' He dropped them on the counter. Jerra saw the sweat coming out of him. 'That's your pay, thassall!'

'Just like that.'

'Silly bastard,' muttered Rosa. 'Yer crazy.'

He snatched up the money and went carefully round the back, past the sweaty, vomitty thing. Near the back door, he stopped and peeled off a two-dollar note.

'Hey, Al!'

Al's head showed.

'What?'

'Money for the Cokes.' He dropped it, swaggeringly, near the head on the floor, hand trembling. 'His is on me.'

'Hey,' called Al. He looked nervous. 'What about him? You can't just leave him there!'

'Your fuckin' customer,' he cried, eyes full, ashamed. 'Serve him.'

Al threw something on the floor. Rosa was sneering.

'Bastard! What am I gonna do with him now, eh?'

'Lock 'im in . . . in – '

Out the door. The stench forced fingers up his nostrils. He leant against the bricks. He wanted to vomit, but there was nothing.

'Crazy bastard!' From inside again. 'Thinks he's tough shit now.'

He pulled jerkily into the driveway. The man next door was harvesting dog turds. Jerra went upstairs, smelling cold pies and roos and puke, thinking of all the caustic one-liners now it was too late. And there was tonight.

'How can they see what they're eating?' she murmured. She seemed happy.

'Yeah.'

'What's wrong?'

'Nothin'.'

Picking her way, the waitress came with the wine, reds jiggling thickly in the bottles. The little gas lantern on the table glimmered on the glass. He couldn't read the label, though he didn't try hard.

'Hope you like Shiraz.'

'Mm.'

'You don't?'

'Eh?'

'The wine.'

'Yeah, fine.'

She pulled back her hair.

'Not the full biscuit tonight, are you?'

He put an elbow on the tablecloth.

'Gimme some plonk. I'll cheer up.'

At other tables, leaning into the yellow gravy light, people tilted glasses, pausing with the glint of cutlery in their hands. The music was thin. Jerra filled his barren throat with wine, watching her neck as she drank. She wore a thin, brown shawl of coarse wool, an open shirt and boots. He felt the hard toes against his jeans. Her eyes were different. Make-up, perhaps, he guessed. Freckles, dusty and fine, glowed on her forehead. No, it wasn't make-up; he had seen those shadows in eyes before; he ignored it.

The waitress returned.

'What are you going to order?' Judy asked, touching his cold fingers.

The waitress held a torch to the menu. It was all a bit silly, and they must have made a mistake with the prices. Whatever happened to the Chinese joints with tile floors and sweet and sour pork for $3.50?

'I dunno,' he said. 'What about you?'

'Umm. Veal Whateveritis. Sounds good.'

'Yeah, but how does it taste?'

'Very good,' said the waitress.

He nodded politely, wondering what the hell about the veal.

'Rack of Lamb. That sounds gruesome enough.' He wasn't hungry.

The waitress snapped her little notebook shut and went off into the darkness.

'Should've had cray, I suppose.'

'Know anything about crayfish dishes?'

'Not much. Only cray a la boil-bust-and-bog-in.'

'Awful things. To look at, I mean. Tell me about your friend.'

'Sean?'

'Yes.'

'Nothing to say, really. Fathers close friends. Grew up together. Best mates. Us the same. You have many friends at school?'

'Not really. Girls aren't really friends at school – just bitches waiting to get you back for this or that. Girls don't make friends; doesn't do much for our image.'

'S'pose you'd know.'

'Yes. I would.' She eased her head back, showing the soft white beneath her chin that ran in a parting curve between the buttons

shining like teeth. Her breasts quivered. 'Bet you spent your childhood in the pinball shops on the beachfront.'

'Oh, off and on. Surfing was big, then.'

'Peroxide your hair?'

'I tried lemons every summer, but it didn't work. Walking round,
smelling like Air-O-Zone. Doesn't get a bloke anywhere, somehow.'

'Not much school, eh?'

'Why? Do I seem stupid?'

She put her glass down.

'I was joking,' he said weakly.

'Oh.'

'Tell you something about crayfish seeing's you're so fasci-
nated by them.'

'Okay.'

'You can float along in a boat some days – a calm day – and
sometimes, if you lift a big piece of floating weed, there'll be a
cray underneath, using it for shelter. They migrate during the
growth season or something, under bits and pieces that give them
shelter. If you keep a shadow over it, the cray won't notice the
difference, and you can just scoop him up into the boat. No one
seems to know much about those buggers. Reckon they travel
hundreds of miles. Like pilgrims, or sumpin'.'

She was watching his hands move, he noticed.

'Ever been crabbing?' he asked, brightening, suddenly self-
conscious.

'Oh, God, yeah.'

'Get bitten, eh?'

'No, but I dreamt it a million times.'

'Great fun, though.'

'Marvellous.' She didn't appear convinced.

'Really hot nights, the mud stinking like an excavated grave-
yard, the lights on the beach, people laughing and talking. Great.'

'Sometimes, even crabs.'

'Boilin' 'em up in big drums on the beach. Cookin' spuds on the
fire. Beer. A girlfriend from school.'

'With braces.'

107

'Him or her?'

'Both, no doubt.'

'Her Dad and others out with the nets. A quick grope on the beach with the Tilley down low. Mud squelching under the tarpaulin.'

'Mm.'

The imprint showing perfectly when packing up to go. Parents' eyebrows. Drop the tarp back down for a sec – shoelaces, yeah, just do the old shoelaces up. Looking down at thongs. The girl giggling nervously.

'Bet she was a younger girl.'

'They.'

'Oh, they? All crawling after you, eh?'

Catching only the distant silhouettes out in the water. Hearing her talk, back on her elbows, brushing mosquitoes, hair lapping back over her shoulders near his feet. Wishing, wishing. Watching all the way up from those little feet, brown thighs shining in the lamplight, to the snug, white shorts. Wishing. And hating that glint on her hand. Imagining the broader mould they would leave, wider scoops in the mud from her buttocks. Sand forced under his toenails. Seeing hers, white shells in a neat row. Wishing *she* had braces. That she wasn't Sean's mum.

'Did you ever have braces?' What was he saying?

'No.'

'Perfect teeth all your life, eh?'

'Yeah.'

Jerra sliced down the bone, stripping away the soft brown meat. He still wasn't hungry, but the wine had hollowed him out, reminding him of how little he had eaten. And the vomiting.

'So where did you go to school?' he asked.

'Methodist Ladies'.'

'Wonder your oldies didn't give you braces, just to show they could afford it.'

'Aren't we the righteous one!'

'Sorry. Was it a girls' school?'

'Girls only at a Ladies' College. You are bright tonight.'

'Like it?'

'You don't like it; you afford it.' She smiled.

'And what did you parents do to get you into a private school?'

'How, not what. They're both doctors with separate practices. Probably didn't know what else to do with their money. Got sick of buying and collecting, and decided to put a few shares into me.'

'Just like that.'

She speared the veal.

'You bet.'

'Did you pay off?'

'Oh, I topped classes and everything, but I think they were expecting something else.'

'Like what?'

'Love. Respect.'

'No chance?'

'I remembered their birthdays and things, but they're hard to love.'

Jerra continued to slice and eat. He was feeling a little better now, stronger, the wine burning in his stomach.

'Are they still together?'

'They go by clauses.' She pressed a fingertip against the bottle. 'Still, there's always a way round what's on paper.' She drank more wine.

Their faces rippled and wavered. Jerra picked at the label on the second bottle and noticed his nails, white in the blue tips of his fingers.

'Be running dry, the way we're going.' He was feeling sad, a little sorry for her, a little sorry for himself.

'Plenty at my place.'

'Yeah.'

'So. You had a friend. Be good to spend a childhood with a special friend.'

'Sometimes it's like putting all your eggs in one basket.'

Outside it had begun to drizzle, slow, floating wisps of moisture settling in the fibres of hair and wool. The VW was only a block away. She kissed him on the neck as he unlocked the door. He could feel the steamy heat beneath the buttons; the shawl was rough on his neck.

'Taking me up on the coffee?'

It was an old, solid house with white stone walls and a large open veranda, like many of the old Cottesloe-Swanbourne fortresses of the forties. The veranda was cluttered with hanging pots, ferns, picture-frames, a rusty tricycle, and a six-foot oak table, buckling in the centre. The outside light was on.

He followed her inside. A long carpeted hallway. On the left, with a lamp in the corner, was the living room, strewn with mats and cushions. Other doors along the hall were closed. Jerra watched the swing of her hair. The kitchen was long and wide. There was a big combustion stove with swing doors, and a long window near the sink which must have overlooked a garden. Twigs and small boughs clawed the glass.

She went to the sink and filled the kettle, dropped wood into the slow-burning fire that murmured when she opened the door, then took off her shawl and threw it over a high-chair.

'Come into the living-room. We can light the fire.'

In the living-room there was a large red-brick fireplace, with pine kindling and large pieces of split jarrah on the hearth. Over the fireplace was a mounted rifle, a weathered Lee-Enfield. Judy knelt at the hearth, sprinkling the wood. Jerra heard the pfff of the wood igniting as he ran a hand over the calloused stock.

'That's better,' she sighed, rubbing her hands. 'Pooh, this kero stinks. Just go and wash my hands.'

When she came back, a glass in each hand, she noticed him running a finger along the rusted sight.

'Like it?' She gave him a glass.

'Hmm?'

'The rifle.'

He sat by the fire.

'Nice 'ol thing. Can't get ammo for them any more.'

'My father gave it to me with the place. Used to take me shooting, sometimes. Took us to the Territory once, shooting buffalo. Shot donkeys once.'

'Shooting as well, eh?'

'When Dad was charitable with his time he used to do lots of things with us.'

'Hunting. Like it?'

Flames lapped round the base of the chimney.

'Better than fishing,' she said. 'Nothing much that beats stalking something big, waiting till you're close, sight him, then bang. He's yours for good. That's real stuff.'

He looked into the fumy reflections of the tumbler.

'Done much hunting?' she asked, poking something further into the flames.

'Only small stuff. Never real game,' he murmured, remembering those quiet drives along country roads with his father, waiting for a rabbit to show.

Ears like two fingers in the air, then the full silhouette as they round the bend. His father murmurs and switches off the engine. Jerra hears the gravel moving as he opens the door, wheels of the ute still rolling. Wedges the barrel in the V-space between the door and the car. Silhouette twitches, tiny head wavering, then settling again. Dirt up behind just before the crack of the .22. His father whispers, 'High and to the left', and he pokes another round in, shaking, expecting the head to bob down any second.

A hit was little different. The head bobbed down anyway. And backwards a bit.

'You don't think hunting's all that good,' she asked idly.

'No. You're not talking about hunting.'

She moved over and sat next to him near the hearth. Her glass was empty on the bricks, blazing with firelight.

'Time for *your* theory, sonny-boy.'

He felt the breath of fire on his face. The whisky scalded the back of his throat.

'You really want to hear?'

'Educate me.'

Hand on his leg. The room warming.

'Animals are different alive and dead,' he began enthusiastically, blindly.

'No prizes for that.'

No moonlight. The rock was cold and hard beneath his buttocks. His father had the whistle in his mouth, sucking quietly. Jerra held the spot, the cord running across the fence to the tractor. Little weeping, shrill sounds came from the whistle.

'Okay, turn it on,' whispered his father. 'See him this time.'

Coals appeared in the scrub about forty yards away.

'There,' murmured Jerra, holding the spot steady on the eyes. Like jewels. Nothing else shone like that. To have one in a little bag, to look at on special occasions, that would be good. To show Sean. Not the rest of the kids. They wouldn't know.

'Off,' said his father. He whistled again. 'He'll come further.'

'Why?' He switched out. The light was heavy, though not as heavy as the little rifle his Dad called the pea-shooter.

'The whistle.'

'What does it do?'

'Sounds like a wounded rabbit. Fox thinks he's got quick tucker.'

'But he hasn't.'

He smiled. They would get this fox. His Dad was smarter.

'On.'

He switched on. Gone. No, they were closer, in the long hair of wild oats to the left. He stood. His father moved behind, resting the slim barrel on Jerra's shoulder. He could feel his father's knees touching the heels of his boots, and smell the oil on the barrel. His father took a long breath. He breathed with him. Crack! in his ear. The lights went out. Only the white circle like a moon on the grass.

Judy waited.

'Explain,' she said, touching his arm.

His palms were damp.

'You said that stalking and the kill were best, with animals. Stalking is good. That's hard; makes you work. But the kill is different. With an animal, killing changes it. With big things. Things that ripple and snort and you can hear them breathing, you're so close.'

'So?'

'No use hunting a buffalo or a roo, because you're hunting something you'll never get. What you get, even with a good kill, is different to what you were after. A roo, I know, won't have that hard, tough look; the eyes are different, like glass marbles. Just a sack of dead meat with blood snotting out the nostrils. A rabbit's like a rag doll when its bladder collapses. Foxes, they're the best thing. You hunt them for the eyes. You get him, the eyes go out, there's just the body of a dog with the tongue out.'

'Why fish? Isn't that the same, catching a big fish?' she said, moving in on him.

'Fishing isn't hunting, either.' He knew now. 'Sitting out of the water, gaffing the sods up, it's luck with a bit of skill. Up to the fish to take the bait. All you do is pull him up, wear him out a bit on the way, and try not to get wet. The fish can rip the hook out, and his lips with it, or surrender.'

And die. With the mate sliding off deep, leaving you with it in your lap, covering the gaff holes.

'So there's nothing worthwhile in hunting?'

'Not animals, but fish – '

'You just said fishing was all luck.'

'Not spearfishing.' He grinned. 'That's hunting. Real hunting.'

'Oh – '

'Odds are nearly even. A few in the fishes' favour.'

'What about aqualung?'

'Slaughter.'

She curled around him. Hot by the fire.

'Now I *know* you're bullshitting.' She giggled. 'All that crap about things different dead.'

'Doesn't apply.'

'Crap! Surrender while you can.'

'A fish is different,' he continued, blurting, trying to explain. 'Doesn't collapse when it dies. The eyes the same, scales the same.

Still a fish. A good kill leaves a small mark in the right spot.
– – – Preserved.'

'Until it goes off.'

'It'll fight, a big fish. Try to drown you if he can.'

She pressed against him.

'I believe it,' he said.

'Mm.' Buttons.

'Do you know about the pearl?'

'Little hard – '

'Something you wouldn't believe.'

'Oh, I – '

'Made out of the part of the brain.' The aggregated life, the distilled knowledge of lifetimes, of ancestors, of travel, of instinct, of things unseen and unknown. His sluggish mind blundered on unaware.

'Silly – '

A hand at the back of his neck.

'The bit he stores and hides – '

'This way.'

' – in the back of his head, hard as – '

'Anything.' She breathed hot.

'And I believe it. Dad – '

'Mind the wall – '

'But lost it.'

'Here.'

'Fell between the boards.'

Floating on his back, the water moved under him. Shirt opened to hot fingertips, scalding, everything. A knee pressed into his side. Ends of hair in his face. Her giggles.

'Bloody fish. Tell me – '

'God – '

'Something nice.'

'No,' he breathed, empty.

'Hmmm?' Hands on him, opening everywhere.

'No! No!'

His face met the scorching breasts as he struggled, hair between his lips. She gasped as he levered her mouth off, flung her aside, groping for the faraway light of the doorway. And no breath.

All down the hall, staggering, he scrabbled with his shirt, chest burning. He tried to cover up, but there were buttons gone. Jumper, he couldn't remember. He wanted to puke. Anything. Opening the door, he sucked the chill deep and it stung all the way down in his chest. Stubbed on the rusty tricycle. Off the veranda.

Kettle screaming.

PART THREE

like men and boys

'I just am, that's all!'
   'No sense in it!'
   'I know.'
   'What are you running away from?' asked his father.
   'Nothing.'
   'Something happened?'
   'Plenty.'
   'Tell us,' pleaded his mother.
   'What the hell can I tell you that you don't know already?'
   'Jerra,' she sobbed. 'We don't know anything.'
   'Then it's the same.'
His father held his arm.
   'Jerra, yer not making sense!'
   'Course I'm bloody not!'
His mother crying on the bookshelves.
   'Tom, what's he done?'
   'Nothing! I got sacked, orright? Here's my board.' He held out
some notes.
   'We don't want that!'
   'What do you want?'
   'Whatever you want.'
   'You can't. It's too late.'

He rolled the canvas tight. Rope lay in coils. He had done it well
in the dark, not sleeping all night. Picking up the box of

cans and cartons, he went for the door.

'Where will you be, then, son?'

'Fishing,' he said. 'Or something.'

'Jerra?' His mother held out her arms.

He slapped the flywire door back.

Boys don't say it.

The VW was nearly full. Next door, the man was starting his mower before breakfast. Drizzle drifted.

Boys don't.

All the way to the sea he could see the collage of city, misted with rain and latticed with sunlight where it penetrated the cloud, gradually losing focus, diminishing in the mirrors as Jerra sat in low gear up the winding hills. Drizzle spotted the windscreen, blurring, but not wetting it enough to use the wipers. At the top of the hill, the labouring VW was eased, and the road wound through hilly pine forests and gravel pits. It rained heavily. The tyres hissed and the wipers slapped spastically on the glass.

'Do you love me, Jerra?'

'Yes.'

Her gown was slipping; a nurse passed, eyebrows lifted.

She always asked before he left. He always felt the eyes on him in the corridors as he left, with her looking after him.

The monotony of pines diminished into hills and thick pastures clogged with huddling grey sheep. Gullies lined with trees furrowed through the hills, and already, in low paddocks by the road, flat black pools lay pocked with rain, fences jutting out with stiff stalks of cut weeds. Cows slapped their tails in the wet. He passed a tractor hub-deep in the dung-like mud. Cold air was piercing the panels of the cabin, and Jerra felt his feet numbing. He remembered the times on the farm when he had stood, barefoot, in the fresh, green cowpats, warming his toes as he squelched.

'I'm old.'

'No.'

'Ugly.'

'No.'

'Do you love me?'

'Yes,' he said.

'Yes. Tell Jerra you said it.'

'Jewel, I am Jerra.'

She smiled uncomprehendingly.

'I am Jerra.'

She was watching him gaily as he plodded down the stairs, defeated.

A roo lay upturned beside the road, legs stiff in the air. Smears of blood disturbed the gravel, picked over by crows and magpies. Pie meat, the poor bastard, he thought.

Listening to the note of the engine, and tapping out its rhythms on the steering wheel, Jerra tried to remember the things he had forgotten to bring, but it was hopeless; he hardly knew what he had, and, as always, he confused this with other trips, other forgotten things, other items to be remembered. He pulled in at Williams, coasting into the Golden Fleece roadhouse with the motor off, and sat for a moment with the silence.

'Yeah?'

A girl in a red parka, with black teeth, at the window. Jerra wound down. It was drizzling.

'Fill it up, thanks.'

She went around to the fuel tank as he stumbled out. His thongs slid over the oily tarmac, spotted with greasy spectrums, as he made his way to the -EN door. He pee-ed into the crap-stained bowl and flushed away the scum of butts and paper. He had seen the flies and smelt this place in the summer, and for a moment the winter was not so bad. The deodorising thing sat on the browning cistern, a sugary, yellow jube.

Outside in the drizzle, he dug his hands into his coat pockets and watched the girl spill petrol down the duco as she tried to force more into the tank. A cow moaned. He got up into the cab shivering, wiped the mist from the windscreen with his hand, and glanced in the back at the jerry cans, the smoky canvas, the blankets, stakes, tins of food, bags and boxes; the handle of the axe and the end of his spear protruded from the hessian bag. He reached over and dragged out a bag of peanuts. He shelled a few and ate them, stuffing the shells into the ashtray, already full with Judy's stinking butts and the foil from Lifesavers.

'Why doesn't he love me, I wonder?'
    She was wandering again, and Jerra picked off a bud, feeling it between his fingertips.
    'He does.'
    'You think I'm an idiot, dear.'
    He pressed the bud.
    'He hates me, I think. Does Jim say things about me?'
    'I don't know.'
    'Sean hates me.'
    'He hates this place.'
    'He doesn't have to live in it.'
    'No,' said Jerra, smiling nervously at the nurse who scurried by at exactly the same time each morning, to watch them.

The girl came back to the window, hands wet with petrol.
    'Six fifty-three.'
    'How much in the tank?'
    'Eh?'
    He gave her the money, noticing the black underneath her nails. When she returned with the change he had the motor running.
    As the country flattened out, opening onto wider slopes of green, the cold crept up from his fingertips, blueing his knuckles. He felt the tyre blow and the van list as he rounded a bend, and he stopped at the gravelly edge of the road. Thongs flicking spots of mud up onto his back, he went round to the rear tyre. He dragged the dusty spare out and rolled it onto its side in the mud. He found the toolbox and left it out on top of the gear in the back. Opening the heavy

jarrah lid, he pulled out the jack and wheelbrace, tossing aside something wrapped in a smelly old flourbag.

The spare on, Jerra wiped the punctured tyre as best he could, shoving it under the canvas. He sat at the edge of the sliding door for a moment, scraping the mud from his jeans, then wiping his hands on the flourbag. Something heavy inside. He pulled it out. Small flakes came off in his palm. The ringbolt without a bolt. Funny old thing. He dropped it back in.

Rain was falling heavier in big thick drops that left welts in the rusty mud. He climbed back into the cab, shaking off the water. It was midday. He shelled a few peanuts, left them in a little pile on the seat beside him, and drove off.

'Come on, read yours.'

They lazed in her backyard. Sean was standing under the hose, cooling off.

'It's your turn, Auntie.'

'That was yesterday.'

'Okay. This is the end of the one I was on last Saturday:

> And so everywhere I go
> I know
> That there's ships and planes
> And football games
> And bubbles to blow.

'What bubbles?'

'Snot.' He grinned.

'Oh.' She laughed palely. 'Jem-Jem, you're so corrupt!'

Echoing.

Clouds gathered choppily over the southern edges of the sky, thicker and darker than the nondescript overcast spreading behind. Rattling across the small white bridges, he caught glimpses of the creeks with that energetic, muddy complexion of winter. Beaufort, Balgarup, Kojonup, Hotham, Crossman, Arth-r, Abba, Orup,

123 𝒥

Kalgan: little white signs, rough-faced with blisters, fighting out of the strangling weeds of the banks. Jerra ate the peanuts slowly, spinning them out. He passed through the one-street towns, hardly slowing down as he whipped past the diagonally parked utes rusting outside the co-ops and pubs.

In a flooded paddock, with the low, weepy-clouded mountains in the background, Jerra noticed a flight of ducks skidding onto the water. He slowed as he neared the paddock, pulling over onto the gravel. A few hundred yards away, the ducks haggled on the water, and he watched them poking their heads into the black, coming up again and again with gobs of mud slushing from their beaks. He shelled a few more peanuts, tearing the brown film that looked like cigarette paper off the kernels, watching the ducks pecking each other behind the neck. He blew the horn and drove off as they lifted away together, a dense cloud, into the grey sky.

> *Petals fall like scales onto my hand,*
> *My love seeps like water through sand,*
> *– Nothing.*

He smiled, feeling his unshaven chin.

'You remember?' she asked.

'Yes.'

They strolled in the yellow sunlight between stiff buds of Geraldton wax, bees hopping from flower to flower.

'Wasn't a very good poem, was it?' she trembled.

'Better than some I've read.'

'But not as good as yours.'

'Better. Yours was true.'

'. . . *And bubbles to blow.*'

He looked away, flushing at the waxed petals. Other women walked by with husbands and children.

It was late in the afternoon when he passed through Albany, its little houses set into the gully between hills. The main street overlooking the shoals of the inner harbour was clogged with cars and children. He parked beneath the shadow of the town hall clock and went into the Wildflower Café and bought some milk, making his way out of town in a light rain that swept the dark bitumen. The hilly roads wound through fences of trees through which Jerra caught glimpses of the Porongorups on his left, and the coastal hills, low and scrubby, to the right. Gradually the hills subsided, and the trees became rugged scrub. Farms were smaller and less frequent. Cleared land was set further back from the road, the kerosene-tin mail boxes gaping in flat scrub with little sign of farmland behind.

'Don't let them, Jerra.' Eyes direct, of a sudden, then gone again, out the window, to the dressing gowns strolling the lawns.

Light weakened and the sun ignited the mirrors. Jerra found a truck bay and parked under some ghost gums. His eyes ached and he was hungry. There was a barbecue fireplace under the trees, and a table with benches screwed onto it, but the ground and the wood in the pile were wet. He climbed over into the back of the van and did his best to separate the mattress from the boxes and bags. He found a can opener and hacked open a can of peaches. He speared them with the end of the opener. They were sweet and soggy in his mouth. The milk burnt cold as it went down. He shelled more of the peanuts. They weren't too bad with the milk, but he was getting sick of them. He left some milk for the morning and drained the sugary juice from the peach tin.

Still drizzling outside. He stuffed the can and the peanut bag into the barbecue and hurried back. As darkness came, the inside of the van warmed with his breath. He found a blanket and lay with his head on his sleeping bag, the heat of the engine underneath his back. It ticked as it cooled. Rain beat on the roof. Dripping from the cab. He had forgotten: the dash leaked. Little drops; one, another, again, more, each a different shape and weight and tone – *drop!*

From his patch of black, words dropped, sank and swam his way, bending, involuting scarry letter-faces, some sounding, others just lighting up, burning into the empty space behind his eyes.

JELLYFISH	BLOOD . . .
BOYS	. . . WITNESS
NO	JERRA
CORRUPT	JEM
DON'T	JEM
CLOVER	JEZ
LEAVES	CRAZY BASTARD

coming and going, streaming out, a bubble trail uncoiling to the invisible silver of the surface.

In the middle of the night, the whole world lit up, as if by an explosion or a fire. A truck engine knocked. He heard it pull in. Darkness returned, then silence. A moment later, Jerra thought the dash had given way altogether, but then the gush stopped and he heard a zipper and footfalls.

He was warm inside the blanket.

He woke in the twilight, and it was cold in parts of the blanket; places that hurt they were so cold. As light pretended to come, shapes and outlines emerged, and he saw the clusters of droplets on the ceiling. His breath, no doubt. Shivering beads, ready to fall at any moment.

The sky was low and heavy. The rain had stopped. No wind, no sound. He staggered out into the cold. The gravel was soft. His breath clouded grey before him. His feet were stiff and heavy with mud as he hobbled round the car, noticing the Kenworth further down the truck-bay. He climbed back inside, scraping the mud from his feet with a stick.

The Veedub spluttered, backfired and growled. Jerra saw a head appear behind the fogged windscreen of the Kenworth as he slid out of the mud and chirked hitting the bitumen.

He passed the turn-off and almost didn't go back. He braked, sliding off into the loose edge, sat for a moment, then reversed up. The dull gravel strip led down to the coastal hills. There was nowhere else.

He slid on the surface. In the gullies, ochre puddles lay across the road. The deeper ones slopped up into the windscreen leaving mud and grit on the glass. Ruts and holes deepened. Jerra slowed down, wincing as the old bus was jarred and shaken crossing the hollows and washouts.

The black sand was hard, packed down with rain, and the tyres ran whispering over, the wide ruts curving up gently to a smooth hump in the middle. Dark wet roots protruded, and grass grew high, rasping the underside of the body. Trees had grown thicker, leafier. Below in the stillness, the sea through the trees was grey and opaque. Boughs and leaves brushed squealing against the fenders and the roof, showering heavy drops on the ground. A bird slapped skyward.

He passed the shack, furred with grass and leaves. He saw the truck in the mirrors as he rolled carefully down the track, avoiding stumps and jags of limestone. A sapling poked through the truck window. He rolled.

NO said the tree.

The clearing was smaller and greener. The thick grass grew in hairy tufts. Black stones lay scattered, some in the clearing, others in the edges of the bush. He turned off. Birds tittered. He got out and unfolded his legs, tasting the salt.

It was a struggle to get the annexe up alone; it had been difficult enough with Sean. Rope bruised his hands and the axe-handle roughened his palms. The ground wasn't quite dry, but he couldn't wait and risk further rain. Because of the sea-winds he knew would come, he faced the annexe away from the beach, behind the van between two thick-trunked gums.

For lunch he ate braised steak from a can. It tasted of gas and fat. Rain looked inevitable later in the afternoon. He gathered wood and shoved it under the VW to dry and, while he still had time, he gathered stones for a fireplace. It puzzled him that the blackened stones from the previous fire had been scattered. He left them alone, foraging in the bush for clean lumps of limestone, avoiding the granite because it often exploded. He set them in a knobbly circle and dug a shallow pit in the centre. Then the rain came, spattering the shivery leaves, and he sat in the annexe stacking food and utensils. Gulls passed over, heading inland with vacant cries.

Rain fell constantly the next day. Jerra sat inside, listening to the pattering on the canvas, drops making animal scampering sounds, trickling softly to the ground down the sides of the annexe, and ate sloppy things cooked on the stove. In the afternoon he made rigs, stringing together hooks and swivels, tasting the whale oil as he held them cold and brassy in his teeth. He decided to fish the lagoon, but turned back, thinking of the drizzle and the cold granite and blue hands. He sat inside, knotting line.

Clover tickled his ears. They couldn't see each other, it was so deep. Above, the tree spread thick and green against the sky, the scratchy gumleaves shining in the sun. Jerra sucked the sweat from his upper lip. He held his thumb tight.

'How's yours?'

'Orright,' said Sean.

'Hurt?'

'No.'

'Mine neither.'

'Hot.'

'Yeah.'

They looked up into the scabby boughs.

'What if a maggie swooped us 'n' pecked our eyes out?'

'Who cares?'

'Yeah, it's okay here.'

'Too hot for maggies.'

'Ya couldn't see, anyhow.'

'Yeah.'

Jerra wiped his thumb on the clover, big flat leaves smearing.

'Gonna tell anyone?'

'Nah,' said Jerra.

'Secret.'

'Yeah.'

'What if we got different blood?'

'Nah, same blood.'

'Is now, anyway.'

'Yep.'

'Here.'

Something cold landed on his chest. A closed safety-pin. He put it in the pocket of his shorts.

'Like Indians,' said Sean.

'Yep.'

'Our Dads did.'

'Dad told me.'

'Mates.'

'Yep.'

Stringing hooks, thumbs on the barbs . . .

His father's face, soft in the lamplight . . .

He was reluctant to go out at all the next day, under the dull skies. Although there was no wind, the air was cold and sharp. Jerra walked down to the beach. The sand was wind-smoothed in flat hummocks and ridges, the sides of the dunes ribbed and fluted on their bald patches. The bay was calm, the water dark. He looked down towards the rocky end of the beach. There were no footprints. He went back up to the clearing, threw some gear into the hessian bag, screwed his spear together, and made for the lagoon.

The water was clear and cold. He floated, stunned, on his chest, letting the streams shoot up his arms and legs inside his wetsuit; he clenched his teeth, head aching, pushing along the almost oily calm of the surface, and under him brown, green, yellow weed stood upright, lank and motionless. The water quickened him, making his movements easier as he felt his arms come alive with gooseflesh. His head burnt and his breath burst sharply from his snorkel. He sucked in the air, burning his throat.

Everything below in sharp focus. Fish hung in thick clusters, like knotted weed. Jerra wafted through the shallows, pulling himself, with his fingers dug in, along the sandy patches of the bottom. Tiny whiting darted away, almost invisible against the sand, and as they went he could see their veins and gut showing through their transparent bodies. He ran his fingers through the sand as he glided along, turning every now and then to see the billowing clouds settling behind. For a few yards he slid along the bottom, nudging the sand with his chin. A garfish passed on the surface above, snooking along with its bill out like an icebreaker.

Following the declivity of the bottom, Jerra moved out to the reef. He surfaced, bffing the water out of his snorkel. He felt it on his legs. Ruts and potholes opened in the carpeted rock. He dived along a gently sloping bank of turf, soft under his hands. Pomfrets scattered, flashing silver and gold. He could have caught one, wide-eyed in his hands as they passed. The trenches in his palms were darkening, and little welts lifted in crinkles where he had swung the axe.

He kicked out to the hulk and hovered, looking hard. Even knowing, it was difficult to see where rock and timber separated. He swam out to the edge of the reef, a hundred yards further out, and floated over, looking down into the pale blue. It was too deep to see bottom, great schools of buffalo bream patrolling, thirty, forty feet further down. He turned back over the reef.

At the entrance of a long, low cave, a group of scalyfins twitched and banked nervously. He came down from behind them, but they were too quick, their green and black flanks gone under the ledges. He poked his head into the cave, no bigger than a forty-four gallon drum. A small squid, all bulbous eyes, floated against the back wall. Nothing to cook it properly with, he left it, quivering, turning its big eye.

Without sunlight, the water was an oily colour, and the reef was dull with even the most flaming reds and oranges of weed appearing cold and faded. A large bream floated over a weed bank. It was harder to see without sun, without silver flashes. The bream was feeding or asleep. Jerra sank to the bottom, letting out quiet burps of air as he stalked through the weed. About five or six feet away, he aimed for the spine behind the gills. The spear flashed, the fish baulked and avoided the prongs. He tried again, but the fish streaked into open water.

It was cold and his jaw ached from clenching. He took out his knife and prised a couple of abalone from the reef, peeling them off with quick flicks that left them twitching for a grip. He held them in his hand as he swam for the flat rock where he had left the gear. The shellfish twitched, their flesh writhing in spasms. He swam without holding them after a few moments, big discs sucking, welded to his palms.

Steam hissed on his shins as he stood closer to the flames, wood cracking and popping. His hands and face and feet were numb, pricking with blood as the fire warmed him. In the bay, the water was still flat as ice.

He gouged the meat from the shells and threw gobs of guts into the flames, watching them sizzle. He found a clean rock and bashed the meat on it with the flat of the axe. Wiping the dust from the pan with his sleeve, Jerra dropped in a pat of butter and melted it over the fire, flames wrapping back and forth. He could smell the hair singeing on the back of his hand. It curled off in little wisps. The pan hot, he dropped the abalone in, watching them buckle and turn in the butter. He fried each side until the milk oozed out and they were the same colour as the butter.

He heard it faintly, but clear.

> Out in the longboats, then sailors,
> Put your backs to the oar,
> Mind a big bull don't come up
> And nail us —
> Or we will be sailin' no more.
> — We will be sailin' no more.

There was no surprise this time; he had been waiting. Jerra saw through the trees but pretended.

'Smells good.'

'For sure.'

'So you came back.'

Jerra scooped the abalone out onto a plate. The pan fizzed on the grass.

'Want one?'

'Oh, no.'

'Only need one. Be a waste.'

The old man scuffed. Jerra went in and got him a stool.

'There you go.'

The old man sat.

'Looks cold, the water. Dunno how you could stand it, this weather.' His hair was thin and plaited with knots, his beard seemed greyer. He wore an oilskin, dried and cracked in the creases, open at the front, stinking of fish. There were two buttons on his shirt, which was bleached almost white.

'Not too bad once you're in. Gets to you after a while, though.' He looked at his purpling hands.

A stink of burning meat from the fire.

'Rotten smell,' said the old man, chewing. 'Never get it out've yer clothes.'

Eating, squeezing hot butter out with each chew.

'What you been doin'?'

Jerra cut a slab of bread and buttered it, giving it to the old man.

'Went back to get a job.'

'Yeah?'

'Got a job an' now I'm back.'

'Doesn't sound too good.' He moulded his rubbery lips around the bread, butter glistening on them.

'Worked in a deli.'

'Why'd you chuck it in?'

'They chucked *me* in. Or out, the silly bastards.'

The old man chewed slowly, his feet rocking inside the crusty boots. His face was dried hard with sun. His eyes were moist and clear under the dry lids, moving from object to object in Jerra's new camp.

'How's this place?'

' 'Asn't changed. Colder with the winter, and wet, but still the same, jus' the same.'

'Hut holding up orright?'

'Leaks a bit, but I fixed the roof with a strip of wire. It'll last long enough.'

Staring into the fire.

'Where's yer mate?' he asked, holding his hands to the heat. His oilskin steamed.

'Working.'

'How is he?'

'Orright, I s'pose. Dunno, really.'

'Any different in the big city?'

'Just the same.' Jerra grinned. 'Still full o' big-mouths.'

The old face creased, whitening in the wrinkles.

'Come down to do a bit of fishin'?'

Jerra nodded, filling the billy.

'Might do a bit.'

'Not much round, really. Buggers 'ave pissed off on me. Nothin' decent for a while.'

'Couple of whiting around.'

'Could be.'

'What about crays? You could make a couple of pots and sink them in holes in the reef.'

'Too dangerous, walkin' out on that reef.'

Jerra put the billy into the flames, hands stinking of burning hair.

'At low ebb, you could wade out and drop them over.'

The old man was looking on, watching the steam rise from the blackened outside of the billy as the metal handle glowed gold and blue and green, pffffing quietly.

'Like a woman,' he murmured.

'Hmm?'

'The fire.'

'How?'

'Dunno. Just is.'

Jerra wondered. Other things, too. Like men and boys.

'Saw a few fish today.'

'Yeah?'

'I was too slow, though.'

'All slow down a bit, this time o' year.'

'What you been living on?'

'Rabbits. A roo every now an' then. There's carrots, radishes, spuds.'

'Wouldn't think anything'd grow in ground like this. Bit sandy, isn't it?'

'Ah, there's a rich patch behind every shed.' The old man laughed. 'Been ripenin' a while.'

Jerra smiled.

'Bury rubbish, anythink that rots. Makes orright dirt. At first it's a bit hard to eat what grows out've yer own shit.'

Jerra laughed.

A SHIT SANDWICH.

'But it's the best stuff,' said the old man.

'Eating the same thing over and over.'

'Right. But it doesn't do too badly. When you've got nothin' else, there's still things that grow out've shit. Doesn't taste so bad, if it's yer own.'

A light wind was dribbling in off the bay.

'Hard living.'

'Brought it on meself.'

'I haven't told anyone.'

'Some people got bad in 'em. More 'n most.'

'Who knows?'

'Me.'

'I mean – '

'But I *do*. Yer can't burn it out've yer on yer own. Some days I've got along the beach with a stick, squashin' crabs on the rocks, poor little bastards. Jus' pin 'em down an' shove the stick through. Crack, an' out comes the froth. They still bite, though, the buggers, even when yer rip the nippers off the body they still get yer an' won't let go. Crazy buggers.'

Jerra poked the billy with a green stick. It would boil soon.

'We all get that,' he said. 'But there's good things.'

'Maybe. Some things are too bad to let any good come any more.'

'Some people never do anything at all. Maybe it's better doing something bad than never doing anything all your life. At least it's trying. You make blues. You gotta try.'

The billy began to rattle in the flames. Holding the stick through the handle, Jerra drew it out and dropped in some tea, watching the brown stuff spread on the water. He poured it into the mugs, a scum of leaves floating on the top.

'Had a mate, used that as a motto. Said yer gotta hit a good patch, sooner or later. It was north, in me younger days. He was jinxed as a three-legged dog, but he kept at it. We was superstitious bastards. He died broke.'

'Maybe he just wasn't any good.'

'Never fished with 'im.'

'Why don't we make a pot and try for the crays?'

'Bloody reef. It's a devil.'

The tea was hot. Jerra stirred lots of sugar into it, seeing it dissolve in the coppery stuff.

Quickened by the wind, the clouds had darkened out in the bay.

'Rain tonight,' he said to the old man who was hunched over by the fire, sucking the hot tea.

He breathed into his mug and finished it.

'I'd better get back.'

'Want some supplies? Plenty of tea, sugar, flour, tinned things.'

'I'm orright.'

Wind ruffled his trousers as he went.

Sunlight glowed in the moisture on the windows. Brilliant strings of beads hung from the van and the trees. Wind rocked the leaves in little tremors and round drops pattered onto the detritus as the sun shifted through the trees, darkening the sky, browning the earth. Through the webbing of boughs and trunks, the ocean glittered, dazzling fingers of light clenching and unclenching. Frosted breath of mist hung in the bush, wavering, the colour of ash.

Jerra pulled on his jumper and greatcoat. The cold gauze of mist burnt his nostrils. Water spilled from the canvas as he opened the flap, and droplets ran down in clusters onto the rough arms of his coat. Leaves were cold and gummy beneath his toes. A tiny bird glanced off the gilt branches of sunlight that forked and tangled in the clearing.

He prodded the ash and coals with a stick. Underneath the ash was white and warm; he felt the heat on his palm.

With a dirty fishing bag under his arm, Jerra stalked across the cold sand, feeling it, almost petrified with cold under his heels, remembering as they numbed the days when he and Sean would beat the sun to the beach, avoiding the morning traffic, and walk across the stiff sand with blue curling toes, surfboards cold glass under their arms. They would sit in the swell with mates, paddling furiously to beat each other to the biggest of the set, feeling the breeze on their faces as they dropped down into the trough, zig-zagging through the swimmers in the bathing area. On big days, after a cyclone had carried too far south, they would paddle out to the reefs that boiled and thundered as they neared.

NO carved in the hard sand. Jerra kicked it over.

The tide was lower than he had seen it. He walked out over the dry reef, over the rocks soft with algae and kelp. The drying weed was beginning to stink. He picked off a couple of small aba-lone and sliced the white meat from the little ear-shaped shells. Mother-of-pearl snatched the sun. Spectrums quivered as he turned it in the light. He punctured a piece of the tough meat with a hook, and cast into a hole in the reef. Green water surged as he watched the sinker and white blob of meat disappear.

As the sun rose further, weed dried and Jerra sat on a flat rock that normally frothed with breaking waves. The hole glugged as the water rose underneath the ledges and slapped ceilings, the edges lined with fleshy clusters of kelp. Whitebait stung the surface like grapeshot.

Wrench on the line. It trembled. He dragged in and it cut into his fingers. The fish came shuddering out of the water, scales lit in the sun. Jerra pulled the hook out, fin spines pricking his palm. The gills flapped as he held the fish up to the sun with its pectorals unfurling. Breaksea cod – black-arsed snapper, his father called them – not much bigger than his hand.

He wet the bag and put the fish in, scales and mucus clammy on the cloth. The tough meat was still on the hook. Cheap way to fish, he thought, as he dropped it into the hole.

A crab marched slowly across the rocks, opening and closing its orange claws. It would make better bait. He held the line with his left hand, caught the crab by its back flipper, and with the knife dashed the claws off and dropped them into the hole. The crab struggled in the bag as he fished. Another bite. A sweep, big as his foot. He held it under his heel as he unthreaded the hook. The sweep was knife-thin, chromed on its tight flanks underneath the black bars. Sweep were one of the best to see underwater, quick and curious.

Jerra sat until the sun was above the hole. Lips and nicks in the grassy rock brightened in the direct sun and, near the surface, heads retracted into the snug dark. He had caught a half-dozen small fish; sweep, some cod, and a leatherjacket. There were no more bites. He scaled and cleaned the fish, slicing neat behind the gills, disconnecting the narrow little heads of the sweep, slitting the turgid sac of the black-arsed snapper, and did what he could with the hide of the leatherjacket. The unravelling guts went into the hole. He took out the crab and put the fish in the bag. He broke it in half, an eye and battery of legs either side, and crushed the shell with his heel. Tobacco-coloured juice ran out. He took the abalone off the hook and sank the barb into half of the crab. There was probably nothing left down there, unless something wandered through, but it would have been a waste not to have used the crab.

He lowered the bait into the hole. Before it hit bottom, the line whipped into the water, the spool chasing it all the way in, zizzing loops, vanishing in the water. He stood for a few minutes with nothing in his hands but a red welt, seeing nothing but the hole.

He wet the bag afresh and picked his way to the beach.

. . . IT'S A DEVIL

That afternoon, Jerra took three of the bigger fish in the bag, and made for the rocks at the other end of the beach. He followed the crowded little marks, and ran a wide perimeter around the beam half-way. There was still a stink, green as ever, in the sand where the seal had been. It would be there a long time yet. Sand cracked under his feet.

No sign of the old man from the front of the humpy, only a humming from somewhere behind, and the gulls in the trees around. He went round the back. In the few yards between the rickety back wall and the bush, there was a moist, black strip of soil, stirred and turned in heavy sods. The old man crouched in a net of flies.

'G'day,' said Jerra, swinging the bag.

He looked up, blood wet on his hands.

'How's things?'

Wiping his knife on a tuft of grass, flies clinging, the old man looked over.

'Not too bad.' Smiling with blood in his beard. 'A good mornin'. Got this big bastard.'

The hindquarters of a roo, fur tarred with blood.

'Not bad goin',' said Jerra, feeling foolish about the headless little fish in the bag. 'A big buck isn't it?'

'Buck orright. Hairy ol' bastard. Snared 'im in the hills. Most of 'em give it a wide miss – smell me on the snare – but this 'ol hopper wasn't the full quid this mornin'. Fall for things like that when you get old.' Flies dug into the corner of his mouth, a twitching scab.

'How'll you keep him?' Jerra asked, eyeing the neck and head on the grass a few feet away, glass eyes open.

'String 'im up in a spud sack an' let 'im bleed for a day or two.'

'It'll go off.'

'This weather? Nah. One fine day in a hundred. Flies only out with the sun.'

The old man ran the knife up the stomach from the anus, letting the coils spill onto the ground. Steam from the opened abdomen.

'One way to get yer hands warm.' He laughed.

A bit revolting, really, smelling the steam, the bowels open. Jerra noticed that the knife had only half a blade, but it looked sharp, very sharp.

'Caught a few fish this morning. Six. Thought you might like a couple. Too many for me on my own.'

'Wouldn't be right.'

'They'll only go off.'

'You got ice?'

'No room.'

Rubbed his bloody beard. He peeled off a section of fur, flesh pink underneath.

'Do you a deal.'

'Orright.'

'I'll take a couple of 'em, and you take some o' this bugger.'

'Fair enough.'

Jerra reached into the bag.

'You don't have to give me the meat, you know.'

'Deal's a deal.'

He lay the smooth, softly boned fish on the grass. Something else in the bag. He pulled out the half-crab.

'Any good to you?'

The old man looked up, a strip of sinew in his teeth.

'Good for the brew.'

'What brew?'

'Good things grow outta shit.'

'That brew.'

'Keep it in a drum up the back. Got all the produce in there. Anything comes to hand. Bled this fella in there, 'smornin'. Drop what's no good in as well, after. All good ammo. Plenty o' rain. Good for the carrots an' spuds.'

'And they grow orright?'

'Enough to keep the scabs off me arse. She always told me to eat me greens, like me mother.' He chuckled. 'No bloody choice now.'

'Was she good?'

The stunted black blade opened flesh in the flank.

'Good lookin', orright. Spent our weddin' night on a boat we borrowed, a launch with a big open afterdeck. Married in December, hot as hell. We slept out in the open on a big kapok under the stars, with some bottles and a sheet.'

139 𝒟

'On a boat.'

'Didn't sleep, that night.'

'And stayed with boats.'

'Reckon we liked 'em better 'n each other. An' her little pianner. Couldn't play it.' He relaxed on his haunches. 'Was a goodun, our boat.'

'Big.'

'Enough for us.'

'And the fish.'

'Yeah, the fish, orright. We lived like bloody royalty. Thought we was the only people in the world. Gawd, I believed in 'eaven, then. But it was a bugger when it went no good. So she had the licker. And her friends in town.'

'Lousy.'

'Nothin' else to keep us from each other's necks. Nothin' to share 'ceptin' the boat. A boat can only be a boat, said and done, only a boat. Not the same. I just couldn't give 'er what she wanted. We went bad. Her worse. But I didn't stop her, she was her own girl. She got what she wanted in town.'

'Hard.'

'An' some days I dunno nothin'.'

Scaly fingers peeled back the limp skin. It sounded like sticking plaster coming off as the old man sliced upwards, holding the stumpy knife like a pencil, and laid two long pink fillets on Jerra's bag.

'There's a fair swap, seein' I've got a weak spot for leatheries.'

''Squits.' He looked at the long tongues of flesh, side by side on the bag.

The old man continued his cutting and peeling.

'Thought you'd go gogglin' today. Good day for it.'

'Bit cold.'

'Not as cold as yesterday.'

'No good yesterday.'

'Get it while yer can. Bad weather comin' soon.'

Gulls stirred, bitching in the trees.

'Take long for a roo to die when you snare it?'

The old man stretched a flap of skin, seeing the sun through it.

'Not if you do a good job. There's ways.'

'What do you do for a snare?'

'Pianner wire.'

'Must be painful as hell.'

'If you make a mess. Bad to mess up an animal. Killin's bad enough without mutilatin'. This one went down with his legs caught, see?' He showed Jerra the raw patches in the fur. 'Lucky I heard 'im go down, or I wouldn't've found him till later in the day. Just slit 'is throat while he was stunned. Didn't take long.'

'Still, a pretty awful way to go, especially if you don't hear. Could lie there for hours.'

'You can only try to be around.'

'And if yer not?'

'Some things 'ave to be done.'

He laid some organs on the grass.

'If yer want 'im bad enough, yer do everything you can and still do the best by him.'

Liver jellyfish-wobbling.

'Ever go into town?'

'Questions.'

'Bloody hard life.' Jerra shrugged.

'Said before.'

'Ever thought about goin' back to town? To live. Normally.'

'This is normal enough.'

'What about when you get too old to look after yourself?'

The old man bit an intestine in half.

'Too old to look after meself?'

Jerra covered his steaks. Flies were bad.

'One day you'll be too old to fish or hunt any more.'

'Reckon I'll know what to do.'

'And you could die trying to think of something.'

'Not too many choices.'

'And just die?'

'Others are dead an' still walkin' around. You know why I won't go back.'

'If anyone had any idea they would've been out years ago.'

'They've been out, orright. They must've seen the driftwood the day they came – wouldn't've known she sank it before – they think I'm drowned, both of us. Sometimes they're right. I take the punishment every day. Why the hell go back for more? Any'ow, they wouldn't make much fuss over the like of her. Better out've the way, for some. One bastard 'specially, if he knew. Why go back for more?'

'And lockin' yourself away here, isn't that runnin' away. Chuckin' it in?'

'Not chuckin' it in. Any'ow look who's tellin' me.'

She kissed him, gown open, by the hedges at the south end of the gardens.

'I've been writing poems, again, Jerra.'

He nodded. It was hard now. She wasn't getting any better. Sometimes she was worse, carrying herself like a queen, dainty in slippers that scuffed the lawn.

'About my babies. The ones you never saw. You never knew them, Jerra. They loved me. Brothers for Sean. He'd have liked brothers I think. His father didn't want them, though. Not even the last one. It was *his*. I was an animal, Jim said. But I was only a mother, Jerra.'

She pulled Jerra to her breast. His tears wet her, but she didn't seem to notice. There was nothing he could say.

'But he doesn't do it on purpose, Jerra, I know it. He couldn't. It hurts.'

He cried.

'My baby,' she whispered.

He looked up. She was smiling. She liked talking about her babies now. Jerra couldn't bear it. He decided, then, in her arms, that he would go away. A job. Anything.

Sun was gone from the trees. It lit the sky over the hills. Smoke and hints of mist hung in the boughs. Jerra sat looking into the fire, smelling the flesh cooking in the pan and pulling his coat about him. The cold shrank even the fire a little, though the flames sprang out at unexpected moments, the greens and blues so pure and inviting that Jerra sometimes longed to touch. A moment later, a tongue of flame would leap out and burn the hairs off his hand.

He turned the curling meat, sizzling in its fat, darkening. It was too fresh to cook. When it began to burn, he took the pan off the fire. It was hot in his mouth, still bleeding, and tough as hide; he could not tear a piece free from the rest. It tasted of smoke and blood. Spitting out what he could, he threw it into the fire with the piece he hadn't cooked, and went for some water.

The tea was strong and scalding. He sat chewing the half-bitter leaves from the bottom of the mug, watching his shadow move in the pearly moonlight. He breathed the cold air deep.

Better out of the way. He wondered about the old man's Annie and whether the old man knew what he was saying. How could anyone be better out of the way? Perhaps he was like all the rest. Sometimes the old man really got his goat.

'Orright, eh?'
  'That's how people get married.'
  She smiled, long legs shining in the sun.
  'Yes.'

He took the ringbolt out of the VW, and sat by the fire, just looking, picking bits off. He hung it on a short branch and looked at it for a while longer.

Then he went to bed.

He would stay down till he exploded; bring it up to know, wrenching it out of its black watery recesses to end the whole thing. The pearls. He wondered.

. . . It's all fisherman's bloody superstition . . .

hunting

Birds were making cautious sounds in the half-light of morning as Jerra carried spear and bag through the trees. His feet were cold under the fleshy wet leaves, and he was hungry.

Smooth rocks colder under his feet. He felt his heels brushing the pores of granite as he hopped from shoulder to shoulder until he came to the flat rock where Sean and he had dived and caught their fish. He undressed slowly and was stung by the air, naked, fumbling in the big hessian bag for the wetsuit. He pulled it up over his legs, damp and mouldy from the last dive. The zip burped all the way up his chest and the black skin was tight on him. Stooping, he clipped the weights on, then the knife on his leg, cinching the little rubber straps over the hairs on his calf.

White feet in the water, he swilled the flippers and pulled them on. He left the flourbag with his clothes in the big brown sack. He wet the mask, spat on the glass, and washed it out. Leaning his head into the water, wetting his hair, feeling the cold fingers run down the back of his neck. He pulled the mask on, snug to his cheeks.

He pushed off into the icy green and it ran down his back inside the wetsuit, gripping him as he floated. The water was shallow with the ebb-tide. In about ten feet of water, Jerra saw the greenish shadow disappear behind a clump of rocks and weed. He dived steep, ears popping. As he neared the place a great tail, like a giant waving frond of weed, lashed out and was gone under a tight ledge.

Jerra surfaced and dived again, but there were only a few small fish staring bubble-eyed. The ledge narrowed into darkness, too small to turn in, probably impossible to get out of. He followed the line of the fissure, gliding on the surface, to where it was obvious. A splattering of rain on the water. Drops perforated the glassy surface.

The crevice gaped in the side, shrouded with the palpitating weed that bristled around it. Jerra pushed down, weed brushing face and arms. Tiny cracks and holes in the encrusted walls shed spines of light into the twilight. On the bottom, the fanning blue-green tail. As Jerra sank closer, it moved into the darkness of a crack. Holding his nose through the mask, he cleared his ears and sank, settling on the bottom. Breath tight in his chest. He circled the flat, curving floor, pulling himself round with his free hand. The bottom moved under his hand. Peering carefully into the cracks, he saw small fish in most. In the biggest crack, under a sagging beam, was the big fish.

It pinned itself against the back of the hole, gills rising and falling, the eye staring roundly, lip glinting as Jerra came in. It stirred. Jerra lunged and slammed the spear into its broad side, but it was too far back from the head. Too far! The fish lurched, buckled, and sprang out of the crack, ramming Jerra up against the far wall, bludgeoning breath out of him. The wall moved, he heard it creak. Pieces of grit fell, and flakes of rotten ply came off as the fish whipped its tail, pectorals and mouth twitching. Scales rasped against him. Frantic, he took out the knife, almost dropping it, and sank it into the soft place behind the gills, and there was blood; thick, oily stuff. It curled in whorls before him as he dug the knife in more, twisting, feeling the blades of pressure turning inside himself.

The great thing went limp, arched its back, sagged, gills pumping. Jerra dragged it up by the gills, his vision pulsating with a galaxy of spots. Feeble kicks.

Surface. Gobs of blood, crimson. Jerra whooped in the air, coughing his own gobs, gasping, treading water hard to keep his head out. He got the head to the surface, flat teeth gleaming. The tail thumped his legs. It was like wrestling in the schoolyard, he heard himself think, crazy with gasping, breathless. The spear bent and the prongs were tearing flesh, barbs exposing white meat under the scales. He thrust a whole hand inside the gill to get a grip and to give the groper pain. The fish steadied. He found the embedded knife somewhere in the body and shoved it in more. It trembled and shuddered, rolling him on his back. He fought to the surface again, screaming with panic, dragging up through the spirals and clouds in the water. The spear broke off, barbs left sunk in the meat. Clubbing him with its tail. Jerra found his feet on the bottom and pinned it to the rocks. Rain falling lightly, ruffling the sack and clothes. As Jerra was dragging it up the flat granite, shaking the water out of his eyes, the fish gave a grunt, snorted up a gout of blood, and died.

Jerra laid it out on the rock, a bellowing in his ears. His nose was bleeding and his hands were cut. Thick streams gushed from the gills and gouges in the side, pooling on the rock. Jerra heard gulls, but didn't look up. The stub jutted from the flank, showing tattered white. He pulled the barbs out, ripping the meat as little as he could, and did his best to close the holes with his hands. He turned the fish over and smoothed the scales of the undamaged side with the back of his hand, feeling the little terraces settle into place. A little silver hook lodged in the upper lip.

He took the knife out and made a deep cut behind the head. He wished he had the old man's stub of a knife as he pushed through cartilage and bone, through the black cavity, and then the flesh of the other side. When the juices had run and gone, he cut around inside the head. He found nothing. Only the grey little brain and the black lining behind the eyes.

He sat back for a moment seeing the turrum of his childhood trembling in his arms, against his chest, and the fish's mate scything loyally through the water beside the boat – just ruffling the flat surface in which Jerra saw his reflected face – until the fish grunted and died and the mate became a shrinking black diamond silhouette diving deep, beyond the limits of breath, with an old fisherman's myth and something of Jerra Nilsam locked in its conical head.

Squabbling, the gulls settled on the rock as he made for the clearing, ignoring the figure moving up the beach.

> *Like water through sand*
> *– Nothing.*

'Didn't have any choice, did I? It was bigger than me, almost. It wasn't easy, you know, it wasn't easy! I beat him!' he yelled at the old man, knowing different.

The old man clenched his fists that were black with dried blood as he paced by the fire.

'Bad enough you hack the poor bastard up; but you just left it there for the bloody bastard seagulls! A beautiful blue thing like that with those sad-lookin' eyes pecked out.'

'I was crook. Had water in me guts!' Jerra couldn't get close enough to the fire. He was freezing and his head pumped.

'An' the fish? You left it with *no* guts!'

'Arr.'

'Eh?'

'I said – '

'So, you got 'im – big deal!'

'Yeah, I – '

'Jus' left 'im out there.'

'Well, what – ?'

'No *head*!'

'Don't be so bloody – '

'With those bastard birds!'

'Shit!' Jerra shivered.

'What are you? Gotta mutilate fish to find out what you want? Why don't you hack yourself open?'

'And what – ' He spat in the fire. 'What the hell sort of animal are *you*? Talk about mutilation! Like burning women! And with what she was carryin'!' He shouted with triumph and dread.

The old man stopped dead and turned to Jerra, eyes wide.

'Yes.' His eyes shrank, withdrawing into his head. 'Yer got a fish, boy.' He kicked a black lump of dirt into the fire and left. Jerra didn't watch him go down to the beach.

He heard the seagulls screeching until well after dark. He would have jumped into the fire, but he was too cold to burn.

The fire almost out, Jerra brought from the van the bundle of letters he had brought with him. He flicked through the envelopes addressed to him without opening any of them, least of all the last in the bundle, the one about the Guy Fawkes night he now knew so well he might have lived it himself. He had been on a fishing boat six hundred miles away from her. By then the letters were not love letters, nor insane poetical screams, but long, sad, friendly letters – kindly, almost – full of her hopeless advice and explanations and reassurances. He read some of it:

. . . was a beautiful craft, Jerra. Your father would have loved it. And I loved it as much as Jim. I can't deny that I convinced myself to love it, but I thought such an hypocrisy worthwhile . . . well, because of Sean and the hope with the new child. I thought that the only important thing, regardless of how I did it, was to be loved.

And the party. Well, the party. We were drunk, drunk with pretence and enthusiasm and reunion and optimism and much fear, no doubt. I was highly regarded by all as the recovered woman, even though I looked repulsively expectant. Expectant. Such a word, dear Jerra. Take note of it. One must always be expectant, but one must not be stupid and mess it up. You only have a right to be expectant if you are doing true things. Do you understand this? I'm not sure I do myself, though I know I have wanted things the wrong way, pretending too much. Oh, we've all cheated so much! It's the way you go about it. And I can say that all too safely now, because I have nothing else to go about. And I have an inkling I will not even go about that properly.

Please excuse this silly talk from an old lady you are (I know) dearly tired of. I wrote this to clear up the matter of Guy Fawkes night because I know Sean believes I lost the baby on purpose. As I started telling you, we were all very drunk – the Watsons, the Courts, all of 'em – and Jim wanted to show off the new boat, and it was after midnight. We went out without a crew. Too far. It was black. I was helplessly burdened, and drunk – I will not pretend I wasn't – and we kept drinking . . .

Jerra did not read on. He knew it well enough. He saw her, heavy and turgid on the deck of the brilliant white vessel and felt for himself the grinding, shrieking collision with the reef, the settling, the jarring rattling her as if to make her spill her burden onto the boards. It was as if he was there. He saw the red lights in the sky, fizzers and rockets cartwheeling red, red, red up into the vast blackness with their spent, smoking carcasses hitting the water with quiet smacks. And Jim calling 'ohgodogodogod!' as if he believed in one other than himself. Jerra felt her breaking up from within, short razors of pain shredding her as she watched the house lights on the beach. The hull shuddering with her. And the screaming. He saw her stricken, pulling on the long bottle shoved in her face for the pain and to shut her up. Eating on the glass . . . The tide rose, edging them off the reef and into the deep, sinking quickly as Jim fired flares up into the sky with all the other gay lights, and was, for once in his life, perfectly ineffectual. Hurrahs and hoots on the beach . . .

Jerra had lived those scenes in his imagination innumerable times. How they reached the beach was beyond imagination and, apparently, beyond her recall.

Jerra rebound the envelopes with the elastic band.

With all her silly talk, all the stupid advice, he thought, all the insane things she dreamt, I'll believe that part for ever. Jerra hated. And he would not forgive – not even her – that grinning slit that cleaved open the skin of her throat which was cracked, black and green, with her seaweed clump of a head half-buried in the sand that the storm had heaved up. On the same beach.

149

'Didn't they know she would?' he called out to the darkness. 'She was gonna go back all the time!'

Green plastic peeled back to show her grins.

'Been in the water a long time,' said the man next to him.

Jim, up the beach in front of the summer house, wept into Jerra's old man's duffel coat. A crowd gathered on the sandhills, perched on the horizon, waiting for the news.

Jerra looked down at the naked legs and scarred, slack belly. A jade tinge to the blown fingers.

'Slit herself and went for a swim,' said the man beside him, adjusting his coat in the drizzle. 'Crazy.'

'Yes,' said Jerra. 'They reckon.'

'Know her?'

'No,' said Jerra.

Gulls hovered. The other man cocked his head at him.

'Not personally, no,' said Jerra at the man. He kept talking after the man went further up the beach where seagulls flagged in the breeze. 'No,' Jerra said, more than once.

He dropped the bundle onto the smoking coals, and until – at length – it ignited, he did not regret it.

the sea-winds

Rain fell all night. Out over the ocean, a thunderstorm cracked and clashed. Lightning lit the inside of the van as Jerra lay awake, shivering under the blankets. The leaves were still chattering at dawn when the sky was dark as wet soil. His hands were fishy, and blood had dried brown under his fingernails. He lay under the blankets all day, getting up only once to leak in the fireplace. The stinking steam rose and made him sick. He wondered again for the first time in a while, why? Was it Jimbo? The booze? Sean? Or was it him? 'No,' he said once, listening to it in the dark. 'She was crazy.' And he knew someone else who was crazy. The old man was, he just knew it.

Just before dark, the rain cleared and he cooked a damper in the coals he rekindled. The damper was doughy and burnt on the outside, but it was hot and it cleared the taste from his mouth.

He slept in bits, chased down into the pale depths by schools of roe, wriggling mucus, green and leering, calling verses he didn't remember.

Dawn, another grey. More damper in the slow fire. The wet ground was almost frozen in places. Still hungry, he put sandshoes on and walked up the track to where the prints of rabbits were most obvious, droppings showing in the damp. He veered into the bush for a warren. If that old fool can do it, he thought . . .

Gathering his snares, he made his way back to camp, holding the

151

rabbit by its ears as he and his father had, letting the stuff run out as he walked. There was sand in its eyes.

With the brown-stained diving knife, he slit the rabbit up from the anus and pulled back the skin, trying to ignore the putrid steam. He drained off some blood, cut the head and paws off, and hung it with a cord from the fork of a tree where the ringbolt hung. Then he collected some firewood and shoved it under the VW to dry. He sat by the fire all morning, drinking tea and pussy-looking soup from a packet, looking up occasionally to the slow drip from the carcass.

Midday. He stoked up the fire and took the skinned carcass down from the tree. He took a stiff piece of fencing wire and ran it up the anus to where the neck had been. He secured it, bending the ends, and sat waiting for the fire to die. On either side of the fire, he sank a forked stick. Waited.

When the fire was ready, the carcass was no longer a rabbit. It had curled pink on the spit, naked and unformed. Coals clucked and hissed as he took it in his hands, running, running in case it whimpered.

Morning was hard and brittle with frost. The stillness of dawn was buffeted by a sharp wind off the ocean. The bay, as Jerra crunched across the sand, was beginning to roughen like gooseflesh, tiny bumps rising from the smooth grey. Horizon and sea were dark, hard to separate.

N O in the sand.

Jerra listened to the shells under his shoes. The wind was making his nose run. His sleeve was rough. His hair, stiff, weedy, rubbed against his neck. He saw handprints, flat knee-marks.

N O again, wobbly and hurried.

Half-way along the beach, ash-white, perched on the bleached beam sticking out of the sand, the old man sat naked and shuddering. As Jerra neared, he saw that the old man's buttocks and feet were blue, and that there were brown stains in his beard, sand all over his body.

'Hey,' cried Jerra. 'What're you doing out here in the cold? You'll bloody freeze to death.'

The old man stared out into the prickling ocean, knuckles bleached, his penis and testicles shrivelled and grey with cold. A shoulder twitched.

'No good sittin' out here. Gonna rain. Go back to your place.'

'Can hear 'em, you know.'

'Eh?'

'Both of 'em blisterin'. An' the boat before . . . never seen anything like it, swimmin' around in the bits 'n' pieces of yer life. An' it's always the junk that floats. Real things're 'eavy. She was racin' me in. She wanted the truck. She wasn't comin' back. I got in first. Gawd yer swim like a bloody fish when yer desp'rate. An' I knocked the livin' crap out of her when she told me 'er . . . condition. Man's a bugger at times, a bugger. She was leavin' in the morning. I give in to her after what I did. An' hit the grog plenty. Can never do the things wanted of yer. Gawd, but she was orright, me Annie . . . '

'Come on!' Jerra tried taking the bony arm, but the old man would not be moved. 'Come on up to the fire, eh?'

'An' I wus burnin' inside . . . I couldn't let 'er go! I *loved*! But . . . she laughed. An' as she wus down there on the beach in that little shack makin' ready for town, I wus up the hill, drinkin' and thinkin' hard . . . '

'Come on up to the fire, eh?'

Creased and shabby in his greying skin, the old man was immovable. Rain began to fall lightly, opening up tiny pores in the sand. Jerra left him there. He'll come up when it really begins to rain, he thought.

He was uncertain how long the old man had sat in the rain. It had been unbearable to watch. Jerra dug himself into the blankets after covering the fire with a piece of tin in case the old man should come up. Rain spattered, sussing on the hot tin in sharp breaths. When the rain finally stopped, Jerra went down to see; but there was no sign, only a windblown set of footprints wobbling all the way to the rocks at the end of the beach.

The wind was much stronger as he trudged through the sand, doing what he could to keep his hair out of his eyes. The sea was

153 𝒟

the colour of spit, bubbling and foaming. He followed the staggering prints to the pile of granite and began to climb around, the spray from the lumbering waves stinging his cheek, leaving little trickles that ran down the back of his neck under the collar of the coat.

From the top of the rocks he could see smoke from the wobbling chimney. Flecks of weed and dried sponge blew up across the sand, and some were pinned to the walls of the humpy.

Hunched over a drum, the old man wore the cracked oilskin and a black cloth cap. Jerra watched from a few yards away as the old man ladled some of the slush onto the dark, turned soil. Gulls fought in the trees. Jerra was upwind and didn't smell it much. The stuff slopped onto the ground and was largely absorbed, leaving small mallee root turds on top of the soil.

The old man looked up. He dropped the ladle, an old saucepan. He came forward a step, squinting at him, then spat and backed away to the drum.

'Won't give me peace. I smelt yer cracklin'. I knew. She tol' me. That's why, not just 'cause o' the boat. Could o' forgiven her, but she never will. An' you?'

No use this time, either, he knew. It was the same.

'Just thought I'd come over and give you a hand with the vegies.'

'Say it.'

'I said – '

'Come on!'

'Geez.' Jerra sighed.

'Arr, yer can't spook me, any more. Yer can piss off, whosever's yer are! Go on!' He reached into the drum.

Something landed in the sand next to Jerra's foot. Another splattered further away. He could smell it, even in the wind. As he walked away he felt one burst on his back. The stink followed him. Back at the camp he scraped it off, but the smell would not go away.

He looked between the gnarled railway sleepers of the jetty down into the dredged green, green that went for ever down. The pearl was there, somewhere at the bottom. He felt his father's breath in his ear; they were both looking and neither said anything.

It was dark and the wind was too strong for him to keep the fire going. He went inside, listening to the canvas rippling and snapping, the flurries of leaves falling onto the roof of the VW. Rain came and he heard gulls floating over, going inland with the wind. Rain pattered, then sprayed and pelted the canvas and Jerra moved what he could into the van, seeing trickles creeping inward from the ground edges of the canvas. He sat by the blue flame of the Primus, heating spaghetti in a can, bleached every now and then by bursts of light from the sky.

Surf thundered above the tearing sound of wind; the creaks of trees and leaves plastered themselves to car and annexe. Before going to bed, he went outside to the angry night and secured all ropes and some loose gear that was out in the open. Rain showed, driving down steeply, in the light of the torch. Ropes sung in the wind, taut and wet. A dark rivulet was coming down the track into the clearing, black pools appearing on the ground.

Jerra went inside and dried. Already the annexe roof was bowed heavy with water that failed to run off. He left it, knowing that the pores in the cloth would open if he touched it. The rain must ease off soon, he thought. The beach would be being eaten by surf. He wondered how the old man's humpy was faring. Jerra pictured him by the fire, babbling wildly, the ply walls shuddering in the storm.

The little notebook opened in his palm: *All the severed men* . . .

It looked at him. He scribbled, stopping occasionally to listen to the wind and rain, surveying what he had written.

> *All the severed men*
> *Clutching themselves*
> *Butchering*
> *– And the guilt.*

He wondered what the stuff it was supposed to be, closed it to have another go tomorrow. It seemed a waste of time.

Warm inside the blankets. He slept a little.

C.J. Dennis, his bird-like grandfather, and a mealy-mouthed Sentimental Bloke pursued him into the depths with lines he only recalled in his sleep.

> *What is the matter wiv me? . . . I dunno.*
> *I got a sorter thing that won't let go*
> *Or be denied –*
> *A feelin' like I want to do a break,*
> *An' stoush creation for some woman's sake.*

It must have been after midnight when he heard the tent-poles collapse. He sat up and saw the roof of the annexe sagging to the ground. Outside in the wind there was the sound of rain on water. Lightning crackled. A lot of water on the ground.

There was no use doing anything until morning. In the distance there was the creaking, grinding sound of a tree falling, falling. He pulled the blanket round. He felt his head going through things, crashing in his ears, a pinging, slapping surge of sounds that drove his head deeper, further under grey water out of the rain and the noise; and he was laughing, singing and finding strings of words that were never strong enough to stay together pinging around in his brain. Deep – *of 'ope an' joy an' forchin destichoot* – and he tasted the bitterness of beer.

The surface returned in choppy waves, bringing the whipping of cloth and wood back into his ears. Breathing hard in struggling gulps, and he spat things before going down again, feeling the sappy weed stroking his face, eating into his cheeks.

Gulping up into the grey again he heard the shrill whistle of wind and the rabbit squeaks of boughs on the paintwork. Morning soon and he would have to clean up the mess.

Jerra saw a lot that night. He sprinted in the dark with screaming in his ears and lights bursting green around him until his vision was reduced to a mottled opaque green like dense foliage. He smelt the bush. It made him drunk, drunk and floating until he was soaring between vast gorges and over water like a great sea-bird. He flew like this for some time before his wings began to fail him, tearing with the pressure of wind. He began to sink. He saw pollard-gloved hands pierced with hooks, and arms outstretched calling 'Jerra!', reaching up through the mottled webbing of net. 'You can't chuck it in!' the old man said, rolling over and over with his tongue out. Flares burst around, forcing Jerra down to the water, green water, and he slid in and cruised like a shark, savaging, feeding off a struggling creature that swam out to sea leaving a red chalk-line like a diligent Gretel. Excited, he plunged his head into weed, plaited, matted strands, found a slit, and furrowed greedily down into the warm sap-green until sated and ashamed. Then in retreat and revulsion, he saw the shredded corpse jaded under plastic and the Sentimental Bloke called out:

> . . . *I'm sick*
> *Of that cheap tart*
> *'Oo chucks 'er carkis at a fella's 'ead*
> *An' mauls 'im . . .Ar! I wish't . . .*

'No!' Jerra cried.

> . . . *that I wus dead! . . .*

He bit his tail turning perfect, frenzied circles, ripping pieces away from himself in fury and frustration and he came to pieces, each tiny piece stabbing the other with knives and safety pins and eyes and words and cactus spines. Something swam slowly past making for the rarified deep – a muscular diamond – secreting tears of grief that became solidified gems encrusting the outside of its skull like the boil-cased face of Job.

His head went tight between his knees as he retracted, wishing for escape, speed, a bigger engine. Blood between his knees, on his legs. A coughing gout. He hugged the beautiful, sleek, dead creature, afraid to follow the muscular diamond into the depths to see. He cried, left with the dead and dying.

'Don't let them make you old before you're young, Jerra,' she said, trembling as he went back down the corridor. 'Don't let them make you give up. You don't have time to get that way.'

He went out into the sunshine.

Hands had been softer, and drier. There was breathing and the exhalation of weeping trees. Glass tinkled, falling like shells and jagged stones. The brace moved on his chest. Fingers bit into him – twigs. Cold flatness on his cheeks; he was floating up against the ceiling. A cough, bubbly with phlegm. Hot breath on his forehead. Ribbons of grey floated past in the breeze. Still outside. Thunder of surf. Then – now and then – a painful travelling. His body contorted, manhandled.

Coughing racked the grey silence again. He might have remembered a lurching dinghy, a boy crying, face turned; but it did not fit. Something solidified under his back.

'Son?'

It shifted the black. The blanket folded back.

'Yer awake?'

The blanket ruffled. More coughing. The overcast lightened.

'Yeah.' Throat dry. Blood, tasting the way it smelled.

'Hurtin'?' The voice reverberated a little.

'Dunno. Yes. Something holding me round the guts.'

'Hmm.'

'How'd you get in? Annexe's a bit of a mess, I think. Bit of a blow last night.'

The old man coughed, apparently uncomfortable.

'Your shack hold up orright?'

A strange twilight. Windows were higher. Only cracks of light coming through. Jerra felt odd.

'It opened up an' blew away,' said the old man.

'What? Gone?'

'I felt water on the bunk first, in the blankets. The roof was leakin' in a few spots an' then it was pissin' down the insides of the walls, down the chimney. Heard that go later. Went outside and the whole lot blew away like a tent. That ol' drum was rollin' around, sprayin' everythin'.'

'Come here to get out of the rain, eh? Thought I heard some noise. Find a blanket orright?'

'You what?' The old man's voice sounded strange again, as if he was taking another crazy turn off on his own.

'Hard findin' yer way in the rain?'

'Bloody oath. Water was up to the sandhills. Thought I was gonna get sucked in, a couple o' times there. In the bush, stuff tumblin' everywhere. An' gettin' you up the track with all the water comin' down, like wadin' upstream.'

He coughed, rattling. 'Heavy bastard you are, too.'

'Hang on – ' It was crazy talk to Jerra who did not understand.

'Oh, you – ' The old man laughed.

'How'd you get here in all – ' Jerra became impatient.

'Stumbled into the tree. Bloody great tree stickin' through yer bus. Crashed through the roof, pinned you. Bloody mess. Bit of a shame about yer bus. An' yer a bit knocked about by the looks of it. Nothin' busted, I don't think.'

What the hell?

'So where are we?'

'The old hut. Up the hill. Nowhere else to go.'

Jerra lay, going through it again. Then the VW is gone, he thought, or maybe the old coot is exaggerating. He decided he would have to see for himself. He could feel the old man next to him on the dusty boards. It hurt under the damp blanket.

'Dawn soon,' Jerra murmured. 'I'll go down an' check the damage.'

The old man wheezed, shuckling up some phlegm.

'Night's only just come.'

Jerra listened to the gentle burr of bark on tin, his back aching. He thought he caught a word or two, but they were gone. It was all beyond him.

'Will you stay here, now the other hut is gone?' he asked a bit later.

'Have to think,' breathed the old man.

'Not much timber around. To rebuild.'

159

'I got this one. Last as long as needs be.'

'Pretty safe up here. No one's gonna look for you.'

'Just can't fight 'em any more, that's all. Just keep goin' till I can't.'

Ocean hammered in the distance.

'Don't s'pose there's anything to eat,' said Jerra. 'Thirsty as hell, too.'

Old man scuffing around in the dust.

'Went down this afternoon and found some things. Matches . . . knife . . . here, some biscuits. Soggy, I expect.'

Jerra ate a couple. They might have been gingernuts.

'Saw that groper, too,' the old man said, carefully.

'Mm.' Jerra closed his eyes.

'Stuck up in the rocks, above the watermark. Crabs been at it.'

'Made a mess o' that. Didn't I?'

'Yeah, a mess.'

'Nearly took me with him.'

'Did good to beat him, I s'pose.' Cough coming from deep within him. 'But not good enough, son.'

'Beat him, didn't I?' said Jerra, suddenly arrogant.

'No.'

'Some things you can't get around. Your words.'

'Yer can have anythink and it'll likely be no good. It's how yer get it and what yer do with it, that's what counts. Havin' it's nothin'. Everybody's got things. It's nothing.' The old man paused and spat. 'Go to sleep. Some water here if you need it.'

Jerra closed his eyes.

'I was after the pearl, you know,' he whispered. 'It didn't have one.'

The old man chuckled in his throat.

'Keep tryin', boy. You 'ad the wrong fish. Spear an open swimmer, they're the ones. Cave fish see nothin'.'

'An open swimmer.'

'They're the ones.'

Morning was a long way.

. . . or see this great fire any more, lest I die

The pool of yellow slag was dry and hard beside the blanket left in a crumpled ball. Green, fleshy leaves protruded through the tin. Out the window, the sky was the colour of dead skin.

Pain was more distant than he anticipated, much of it from lying on the wooden floor so long. His back was tight. On his forehead there was open skin, hard already with drying, and he found grazes on his arms, and a thin pain – like little barbs – in his hip. He limped out into the pale light.

Guttered with washouts, the sand track wound slowly – NO faint and puffy wound in the bark – until he saw the knotted masses of foliage in the clearing; a shred of canvas impaled on a branch; vomitty flour pooled on the mud. Wide black puddles reflected the thin clouds. The VW, toppling on its side, was fused to a thick gum, fenders crushed. Unmelted hailstones of glass lay on the ground. He peered in. The steering column a splintered tangle; panels buckled; boxes spilling. Black blood, stinging scent of eucalyptus, wet blankets. He reached in for his shoes. He found two oranges and his coat. Matches. The shoes might have been anywhere. He put the oranges in the pockets of his coat. The old man will be hungry, he thought, wondering where he might be.

Weed and shells were strewn up on the sand; heaps of piled weed, buzzing with little insects. The bottoms of the dunes were eaten away and deep gouges ran part of the way up the beach. Jerra heard the gulls. The old man was not here.

161 𝒯

He went up the track, stumbling barefoot in the deep open veins in the mud, pulling his coat tight around him, the shit-stink following. Bird noises. He thought perhaps the old man would be back at the shack. Gulls hahed high in the trees. Others were skirting the treetops, crowding in.

'Ah, bastards.'

He cut into the bush.

The gulls moved back without blinking when he came close. The old man's face was in the mud, feet in the air, ankles pecked raw where his trousers had crept up, skin open, sunk with piano wire that gleamed dull. A little puddle of blood and mucus bathing the old face. The ringbolt on the ground, next to the puddle.

Jerra sat keeping the birds away for a while. He knew what he would do.

A single witness shall not prevail . . .

On the beach, he wrapped the old man in the tattered canvas sheets. He tied his diving weights around the middle, threaded the ring through. He undressed. He took the old man's boots off the cooling feet. He waded out to the shallow part of the reef, the icy water gripping his shins. Beneath his numbing feet, the fur of algae yielded softly. He steered the bundle out stopping every few moments to unsnag it, until he manoeuvred it over a hole, using the ring at the waist as a handle, and lowered it over the edge, watching it sink slowly into the green, grey hole. The water stung his cuts. He watched the green.

Seagulls were gathering on the water as he pulled his clothes back over his blue limbs. The old man's boots were rank, but soft inside. He went up to the clearing. Digging into the mess he found sultanas, and socks for the boots. Packets, boxes, coils, blankets spilling. Birds in the trees, mostly gulls, were showing their pink tongues, one close in the fallen tree that crushed the VW. It laughed at him with those red Sean-eyes, squinting, edging closer.

'Bugger off, yer bastards!' he yelled.

The gull came closer. Blinking.

Jerra lit a match, smelling the dead breath of its smoke, dropped it into the fuel tank and ran.

ALSO BY TIM WINTON IN PENGUIN

Shallows

Whales have always been the life-force of Angelus, a small town on the south coast of Western Australia. Their annual passing defines the rhythms of a life where little changes, and the town depends on their carcasses. So when the battle begins on the beaches outside the town, and when Queenie Cookson, a local girl, joins the Greenies to make amends for the crimes of her whaling ancestors, it can only throw everything into chaos.

'The prose and learning may even stand up to Melville himself . . . the elegance of language, the grandeur of nature being described – all this is dazzling, dazzling. It makes the heart pound.'

Los Angeles Times

'*Shallows*, his finest work to date, is more than a passionate meditation on the tragedy of whaling; it is in some ways a minimalist *Moby Dick*, a questioning of the ways of God to man and of man to God.'

A.P. Riemer, *Sydney Morning Herald*

'*Shallows* is a profound and inspiring work of fiction.'

The Age

That Eye, the Sky

Ort knows the sky is watching. He knows what it means to watch; he spends long hours listening at doors and peering through cracks. Things are terribly wrong. His father is withering away, his sister is consumed by hatred, his grandmother is all inside herself, and his mother, a flower-child of the 1960s, is brave, but helpless. Then a strange man appears at their door.

That Eye, the Sky is about love, about a boy's vision of the world beyond, about the blurry distinctions between the natural and the supernatural. All this, and more, begins at the moment the ute driven by Ort Flack's father ploughs into a roadside tree, throwing the whole world out of kilter.

'A wrenching story that proves that love like Ort's can prevail against hell itself.'

Publishers Weekly

'The best book about a boy I've read since *Huckleberry Finn*.'
Robyn Stone, *Sydney Morning Herald*

'A story of generosity, insight and originality.'

Weekend Australian

ALSO BY TIM WINTON IN PENGUIN

Cloudstreet

From separate catastrophes two rural families flee to the city and find themselves sharing a great, breathing, shuddering joint called Cloudstreet, where they begin their lives again from scratch. For twenty years they roister and rankle, laugh and curse until the roof over their heads becomes a home for their hearts.

Tim Winton's funny, sprawling saga is an epic novel of love and acceptance. Winner of the Miles Franklin and NBC Awards in Australia, *Cloudstreet* is a celebration of people, places and rhythms which has fuelled imaginations world-wide.

'*Cloudstreet* gets you inside the very skin of post-war working-class Australians the way Joyce makes you feel like a turn-of-the-century Dubliner . . . People get up from where they have fallen, they try, they keep on. Above all, they laugh at themselves, sometimes bitterly, but much more often riotously. *Cloudstreet* is a hilarious book.'

Elizabeth Ward, *The Washington Post*

'It is, I suspect, a masterpiece.'

Veronica Brady, *West Australian*

'Nothing short of magnificent . . . a wonderful read.'

Andrew Yule, *Time Out*